navigatio

For David

With love

[signature]

December 2000

navigatio

Alison Croggon

Black Pepper

© Alison Croggon 1996

First published by *Black Pepper*
403 St Georges Road, North Fitzroy, Victoria 3068

All rights reserved

National Library of Australia
Catalogue-in-Publication data:

Croggon, Alison , 1962 - .
 Navigatio.

 ISBN 1 876 044 09 8.

 I. Title.

A823.3

Cover design: Gail Hannah

 This project has been assisted by the Commonwealth Government through the Australia Council, its art funding and advisory body.

Printed and bound by Currency Productions
79 Leveson Street, North Melbourne, Victoria 3051

Alison Croggon was born in 1962 and has three children. She trained as a journalist on the Melbourne *Herald* and her work includes poetry, plays, libretti, translations, editing and criticism. Her first book of poems, *This is the Stone*, was published in 1991 and won the Anne Elder and Dame Mary Gilmore Prizes that year. Her opera *The Burrow*, with score by Michael Smetanin, premiered at the Perth Festival in 1994 to critical acclaim and had seasons in Sydney and Melbourne. Her play *Lenz* premieres at the 1996 Melbourne Festival, produced by the Mene Mene Theatre Company. She has recently completed the libretto for *Gauguin*, her second opera with Michael Smetanin, which will be produced in 1997. She is currently poetry editor for *Voices* and her second collection of poems will be published by Black Pepper next year. *Navigatio* is her first novel.

Not every Thought to every Thought succeeds indifferently. All Fancies are Motions within us, reliques of those made in the Sense: And those Motions that immediately succeeded one another in the sense, continue also together after Sense.... But because in sense, to one and the same thing perceived, sometimes one thing, sometimes another succeedeth, it comes to passe in time, that in the Imagining of anything, there is no certainty what we shall Imagine next; *Onely this is certain, it shall be something that succeeded the same before, at one time or another.*

Thomas Hobbes, *Leviathan*

Contents

Prologue		1
I	Arcadia	5
II	Anaesthesia	15
III	Analects	23
IV	Adelaida	35
V	Abidings	43
VI	Ananke	55
VII	Africa	65
VIII	Angel	77
IX	Accounts	89
X	Apeiron	99

Prologue

Begin at the beginning, said the Red King. But no beginning is ever the real one, there is always something before that...

I knew, all my childhood, that I was my father's favourite daughter. The betrayals of adulthood, the cruelties and indifference, do not change this, but endow it with the intolerability of paradox. My weaknesses, my fears, my dishonesties, the defining hurts of my life, are my inheritance from him: and these words. Particularly these words.

I want to migrate forever from these shadowlands where speaking is not possible because the darkness swallows every syllable before it can be uttered, this realm that ate up my parents. Each step takes me further into shadow, into the impossibility of speaking. But I must persist.

My father, also, desired a place to speak freely: he tore himself and his family out of the old country where only the privileged could be heard and brought us to a place where a possibility of freedom still lingered, where a man could walk without the burden of history on his shoulders. But his flight across twelve thousand miles of ocean wasn't enough to strip the history out of our bones. It came with us, a sinew flexing secretly within us, a black vine which contracted all the space around us to a bewildering tangle of choking branches: so that here, too, we could not speak.

My father preserved our writings and drawings, and at night, as I lay in bed, told me the tale of Perseus and his winged boots, and recited "My name is Ozymandias, King of Kings!" in the shower so that the great rhythms fell into my mind and became part of me. He made, also, the great scrapbook of beautiful pictures - curious postcards from Chile made of beaten copper, advent calenders, photographs of church windows cut out of magazines - with its huge brown pages bound with brass bolts between large boards covered with a luxuriously textured, flesh-coloured fabric. The pages had to be turned one by one, or they would crease under their own weight.

For most of my childhood he was absent, travelling in Chile or Canada or working at the mine. I am sometimes afraid that I can understand nothing except absence, that his weaknesses are my weaknesses, that, despite all my striving, I am truly my father's daughter.

Dress over ankles, head over arse,
Alice fell into the looking glass.

On my desk is a photograph of my mother. I am older now than she was when it was taken: it dates from Cornwall, when I was six. It shows a pretty, neat young woman in a prim, high-necked tailored dress (I remember the dress - it was grey and the polka-dotted tie was navy blue). Her hair is swept back into a bun, revealing fine features: high cheekbones and forehead, a firm, almost square jaw. Her eyebrows are neatly plucked, with a wide space between them, and carefully pencilled over; she wears pale lipstick and almost no eye makeup. She is smiling, but restrainedly, and her eyes look somewhere to the right of the photographer's shoulder. The shyness in her eyes makes her look younger than she is and seems to release a brightness of expression otherwise hidden in her face. There is a slightly awkward tension in her shoulders which unsettles her poise.

At that time, she had probably been married to my father for about seven years.

There is a ship which folds time around it like a scarf of wind. It is made of wood, to signify its status as an anachronism, an object of nostalgia and derision and desire, and it heaves over the black waves with its rigging straining and creaking. Its belly swells with voices which bleed out into the night and are forgotten, which matter only to themselves, which can never be erased from that secret book in which all eternal things are inscribed and which anyone can read, if they possess the necessary simplicity, the necessary love...

We feel bitter when we encounter this ship: it carries all our pettiness, our cowardice, our nightmares, our futile tears, all the dank unnameable acts which haunt us below our memories. But sometimes the holystoned deck glistens with a whiteness our eyes cannot register, and above in the sails we hear the sound of wings, as if the sky were pulsing at last with our failed and betrayed divinity.

I Arcadia

Once upon a time there was a castle built of yellow stone, with a rampart that dropped sheer into the blue sea. The sky had no clouds and was pale and edgeless, like a robin's egg.

Once there was a woman who stood on the rampart with her three small daughters. The sun struck the stone and rebounded into her eyes, blinding her. She was afraid her littlest girl would climb over the rampart and fall into the sea.

Near the castle was a park. The woman sat beneath a tree and watched her daughters playing. The breezes stroked her mouth and thighs and carried her off to sleep. The three little girls wandered off between the beds of flowers into a maze of paths. When the woman woke up, they had all disappeared...

Once upon a time there was a big house of granite with a greenhouse and a bamboo grove and a winding pathway set with millstones. In the garden were ancient rhododendrons which dropped their heavy flowers like bells of blood onto the black earth. The little girls would run down the path to the laurel tree to pick bay leaves for their mother. Around the garden was a stone wall and in the wall was a cast-iron gate, painted midnight blue.

The garden is stippled with the rich honey light of autumn, which ripples over the children as they chase one another across the lawn and fall, giggling and breathless, underneath the window which opens out of the sitting room. She is watching from the window and, although they cannot see her, they are aware of her gaze, which is reflected in the red and purple berries on the trees and the scented eyes of flowers and the quick flickerings of light scattered by the birds.

For the youngest child, this garden is the whole world. The middle-sized child is planning to run away on her tricycle. For the oldest, it is a place which can be measured against other places: she knows it as a haven, a cradle, a temple, an earth of return and celebration. Greenness surprised her, when she first arrived, she had never imagined the possibility of the lush fields, up to her knees in grass as soft as her own skin, or the abundant fountains of lilac flowers: these things were like new sight, and the country of her babyhood shrank to the small black and white photographs pasted in the thick family album. Because of this comparison, she knows herself to be happy.

The mother watches the children and hears without hearing the low voices of the garden underneath their shouts and laughter. She leans her brow against the windowpane and lets her body fill with wordlessness, a radiance which dissolves the contours of her body and sets her heart beating in everything around her so that her self is no longer the self she knows but faceless and tender as the light.

The youngest child looks up and sees her and lifts her arms towards her, so the mother bends through the window and blows her a kiss. The little girl claps and shouts and runs to hide behind a shrub, peering comically from behind it and withdrawing, scarcely human or substantial, an embodiment of the breeze which moves in little jumps and startles through the leaves. The other children run to the shrub and they crouch down, examining a leaf or a snail or a beetle, out of sight.

Released, the woman returns to her sewing. She is making a dress for her youngest daughter. She is still inhabited by wordlessness, knowing without looking how the fabric runs surely through her fingers, effortlessly straight, and how the cotton gathers evenly for the skirt and around the armholes, how precisely the scissors glide through the cloth. Her face is intent and serene as she draws to herself all the sounds of the house and garden, monitoring on subtle webs the actions of her children, the angle of the sun slanting over the house until suppertime.

Soon she will go to her kitchen and draw the roast lamb out of the oven. She will send her oldest child to the back garden to gather mint and chop it with sugar and vinegar to make mint sauce, and mash the boiled potatoes with butter and milk and pepper and pour white sauce over the cauliflower heads and put them into the oven to brown. Perhaps she will put Handel's *Water Music* on the gramophone, or perhaps the children will be watching *Dr Who* in the breakfast room, unconsciously creeping closer and closer to the television screen, their eyes wide with pleasurable horror. She will set the china on the table and they will eat, orderly and hungry, and when they're finished she'll take out of the oven the golden rice pudding, brown and crackling with cream and sugar at the edges of the ribbed iron pan. Then she will bathe each of them, washing their hair carefully and cleaning their ears, and dress them in pyjamas and put them into their beds. The house will hold their breathing in its immense quiet like a quivering fountain and she will hear it downstairs, as she sits by the fire, as her skin ripples in the imperceptible currents of their sleep.

We referred to each other, between ourselves, by the initials of our names: F, C and A. To each other we were the known world, givens more certain than the constellations, and our relationships within these certainties were casual and cruel, a play of shifting alliances and merciless competition. Above us loomed the figure of our mother, all-powerful, beautiful, capricious, stern, the object of our adoration and fear and passionate jealousies.

In my memories of England, my sisters are faceless presences, as if they were parts of myself. I don't know whether this simply reflects the self-absorption of childhood. How does one trace the origin of a fracture in oneself? We still trouble one another, raising unsettling mirrors which flash into our different presents those ancient feuds and alliances, and with them the constant, violent desire to be ourselves, separate at last from these insistent identifications with which we are branded, separate from the histories which have shaped us and which seem to trap us again and again in their sad repetitions of failure.

I have a black and white photograph of three little girls, taken that day at Lisbon when we got lost in the park. We are sitting underneath some stylised metal toadstools in the middle of a garden of flowers. Behind us runs a broad gravel path. Behind that, there is a stand of trees through which you can see a patch of white, which might be a building. It is warm, because we are wearing light cotton dresses and sandals. It is just before my seventh birthday. C is four and F is three.

F, the youngest, is our mother's favourite child. She has the fairytale advantage of having two elder sisters and knows herself to be the most beautiful, the best, the real princess. A shadow bisects her face and she stares through it with an unweighable expression: cautious, sceptical, self-assured. She is severely pigeon-toed and holds herself with a hint of spasticity, running with a peculiar, stooping gait which we would later often parody. F is the one whose hair is never cut, and it is natural for us to admire the tendrils around her forehead with their glints of red and blonde, as it is also natural that C's black hair is cut short, with a blunt fringe, and that I should be nondescriptly in between, with brown, straight, shoulder-length hair.

C peeps over my shoulder, her thin body incandescent with a kinetic energy, a strikingly pretty child with unusually large hazel eyes and a sharp, elfin face. In the cosmology of our family, C is the lone planet travelling an elliptical orbit. She is the child who takes after my father's family, unlike F and I, as if our very bodies were replicating the feuds of an earlier generation. C's face is less hidden than F's or mine and her eyes flash open to the camera, voluble and mischievous.

I am the most invisible. My eyes are completely hidden from the camera. I cloak myself already with the anonymity of a writer, already I see my thoughts as words crossing over my inner vision. The gap between myself and I has become apparent to me: I have just been torn from my Eden, and God has been banished from my sight.

My mother hungered for a home with the passion of the homeless. She was born during the War and so could not remember, as her older brothers did, that mythical time when there had been money. A time came when all the money was lost, when serially they left the houses they lived in, leaving behind them gold candlesticks in the garage and boxes of photographs and letters and spoons, shedding their history with a kind of reticent shame.

Although they considered themselves poor, my grandparents ensured my mother had a governess. She was taught the infinite gradations which alerted the initiated to the recognition of *ourselves*, the nuances of speech and deportment and vocabulary which were so much more than manners: a way of being and perceiving, a cool assumption of authority in which the determining factor was control of oneself and in which any ostentatious display of power was a confession of impotence. One behaved *naturally*, which is to say as unnaturally as possible: one looked relaxed eating with one's elbows jammed against one's ribs, and gnawed bones at the table without the slightest trace of discomfort, and was extremely polite, in particular, to anyone one considered beneath one, and preferred the lower classes to the middle classes, who were considered grasping and vulgar. All this was only possible with the grace of hereditary habit and a secure knowledge of one's own people.

This was the ideal my mother attempted to marry with her longing for a home. It was the ideal which rotted in the lascivious face of my grandfather, dying of asthma in a council flat in Falmouth with his quiet, white-haired wife drinking steadily to maintain her air of serene indifference, trapped inside mean white walls stained urine-yellow with years and years of cigarettes. Even before then, it was easy to despise my grandparents, the decadent remains of a corrupt and collapsed class.

The house was old, three hundred years old. Once it had been the core of a farm, and the slate-flagged courtyard outside the kitchen led, as now, to a vegetable garden, where rows of poles held up the vining weight of peas and broad beans, and canes held raspberries and blackcurrants, and lettuces concealed their white hearts in coarse leaves. Its stern Georgian frontage had looked out over fields of luxuriant grass hidden behind earthed stone hedges that were softened by ragged robin and cowslip and primroses, and in the fields had been pigs and geese and the heavy-limbed working horses and slim-hipped Jersey cows and, horned and flanked with dark, matted hair, one bull... But the town ate up the fields and the farmers died and at last the house, forsaken and shabby, waited for my mother to console it with her wallpapers and white paint and wax polish and sandpaper.

She went to the farmers she knew and asked them for the hewn granite drinking troughs which were then being thrown out in favour of modern concrete: and inside them she grew miniature gardens of cacti and dwarf roses. She begged the millstones from an old mill and set them, solid granite mandalas, into the path which led up from the gate. She plundered junk shops for cheap Edwardian and Victorian furniture and restored each piece - a pair of nursing chairs with green cushions and spindly turned legs, a mahogany sideboard which she found in a chicken coop, white with droppings, for ten shillings, an oaken bow-fronted chest of drawers, which was later lost in storage, and cottage chairs and settles and a graceful Regency table. We regarded the furniture with a proper awe, respecting each piece in its given place, for we were very well-behaved little girls. Like the furniture, we were a product of my mother's hard work.

Gradually, we inhabited the house... and where men had stamped and scraped the mud off their boots and whistled to the dogs which crouched, flat-eared, on a piece of sacking under the wall, where chickens had prowled and stabbed for grain or beetles and cats had slunk warily along the flags towards a tin plate of milk, we held our childish conferences and took sandwiches and apples for picnics with our dolls and swung our legs on the low stone wall, from which F fell once, holding a saucer that broke and cut her across the eyebrow, leaving a scar... the back porch bulged with sou'westers and gumboots and the cold friendly noses of dogs, and C fell there once and broke her thigh and her leg had to be encased in plaster from ankle to hip... and in the greenhouse, grown over with mysterious inherited plants, I would play with the green water in the fishtank and scrape patterns on the brown-green glass and pour from a toy tin teapot so the water made a sound like urinating... the house skinned our knees and bruised our hands and cut us with its edges, and gave us nests to discover in the bamboo grove, and the ancient black toad which lived in the walls around the back lawn like a benign spirit, dry-skinned and slack and heavy, and the smart black beetles running over the slate and the woodlice quivering their white legs under the flat stones...

I often dream of buildings: delapidated mansions with tarnished velvet curtains and galleries that lead nowhere or look out over indeterminate darknesses: or I dream I am a theatre, in which an opera of mine is about to open, but there are two or three or four theatres with foyers which have indecipherable signs on the walls and I am never in the right place: or I am a warehouse, in which a saint is living, and in his shower is a mural, constantly changing, which depicts the Apocalypse, and after the Apocalypse, a giant stone hand standing out of the desert, the City of God, and in its ring finger is an eye: and a broad, scuffed flight of stairs leads down to the basement, and at the bottom of the basement, into which I am chased by a man who wants to murder me, a man I love, is a steel door through which I cannot pass.

From plenitude, an inheritance of fragments: from the immediacy of presence, a half-life of exile from ourselves: from the homeland, the rank stench of decay: from the being of God, non-being: from the mother, sorrow: from the father, absence.

I don't know what legacy I can give my daughter. Too much has been broken or lost to allow me to speak of tradition or certainty. I wish for her a clear space where she might grow unblighted and learn her strength. But I am unable to make such a place for her, except in certain rare moments, when the shell of my self-absorption cracks open and my face is open to her...

And it seems to me miraculous that another human being could love me as my daughter does, when she grants me the pure action of her kiss. And perhaps this is the sum of my labour: to find, amid the rubble of illusions, the real kiss that always lay there, unbroken and wholly itself.

II Anaesthesia

If I am calm and speak sweet and low, all womanly the ocean will bear me safely on its breast and my little chicks tucked in around me will feel the soft feathers of my voice and know a home. They are so small to ride so large a sea... How frightening the world became when I gave it hostage!

I am so tired. I hope they stay sleeping, perhaps I can keep writing, but it's hard in here, the shadows are crazy, flinging themselves around the walls. I'm so tired. But this scribble grants me a little peace.

16th June 1869
HMS Fidelis

My dear William

I miss you all so terribly already and we are scarcely past Plymouth! I felt as if a part of me was dying as the docks slipped away. The voyage even so far feels like a nightmare - stuck in a tiny cabin with three small children and no help is trying, to say the least. I am attempting to keep my composure, for their sake, but I shall have to do better than I am. Perhaps as I become used to this place things will become easier to bear. I feel I have done wrong in agreeing to wrench my family from their home where they were so happy in order to travel to a wild place of which we know almost nothing. But Roger brooks no disobedience. Forgive my complaints, I am very unhappy! Catherine has been fretful and restive the entire time, enough to make me thankful for Adelaida's muteness: and Fanny has been most horribly sick. I don't understand how the passengers manage in steerage; I am doing so badly, and I am in relative luxury. Down there they have to cook their own food and there is little or no privacy. I saw a woman trying to wash some napkins in a bucket on deck: a lieutenant came and was about to throw them overboard, until I intervened. I have seldom felt so angry. The woman, whose name is Agnes Clare, told me what it was like. She has a colicky baby and is very afraid that another passenger, who sleeps nearby, might smother it to stop it from crying. She is a widow and is travelling to her sister, who runs a hotel in a town called Ballaarat. Her stoicism made me feel ashamed. I would like to help her, but fear I might offend her. Because I have been talking to her and no doubt because I am a woman on my own, some of the other passengers do not acknowledge my greetings. They are so petty: and yet I cannot help feeling hurt. The thought of spending four months on this ship oppresses me as much as the fear of what I might find at the end of the voyage. Tonight I don't know if I can bear it, which is why, my dear brother, you are shouldering the burden of my complaints. There is no one I can speak to here who will understand me. How I wish we could go out to a dance, and you could scribble all those silly notes over my card, as you used to! I thought marriage would be like that, only more so. How wrong I was! But here I am, complaining again. I shall write again soon, in a lighter mood, I hope. Meanwhile think of your sister, who misses you so much and so needs your malicious remarks to make her laugh.

With all my love, Jackie

I read once of a painter who died on a tropical island where he had exiled himself, because he could stand the ignoble merchants of Europe no longer, because he saw in the savages a possibility of uncorrupted human beauty. And they found his last unfinished painting and it was - a snowscape!

How terrible, to die of longing for that which destroys one. Or to wake blankly from a dream so compelling that it seemed real, to find, once again, oneself...

Somehow, in the muddle of everything, I lost myself. I was a girl, and then I was a woman, and then I was married and I belonged to someone else. But I thought I was someone, once. I don't know how it happened. Maybe I forgot something important, or maybe I was made to forget. Or maybe that is how things are when you're grown up. But I keep thinking, if only I could remember, something - I don't know what! - maybe - like a precious button that I had when I was a little girl, a gold button with a coat of arms on it, that I hid in a secret place and was just mine - something like that - but I know it's not that, it's just like that. And if only I could remember it, then I'd be free. But it's so absurd, to be thinking like this. Imagine if someone read this! How foolish I would feel!

16th June 1869
HMS Fidelis

My dear Husband

The voyage so far has been very pleasant and the children are all well. Adelaida is exhibiting signs of a slight Cough and Catherina has been worrisome, as usual. Fanny has been most terribly Seasick, which has led to a certain amount of disruption in the cabin, but nevertheless we are all cheerful.

It is difficult to find any Acquaintance on the ship, apart from amongst the Officers. A certain Mr Haricot very kindly took Fanny on his lap at dinner yesterday night but the poor thing disgraced herself! Mr Haricot was very embarrassed. However, without Help I do not feel I can leave the children behind in the cabin, and so they must come with me.

The Weather has been mostly fine, apart from a slight gale a day ago, which alarmed us all exceedingly. We are looking forward to docking in Melbourne very much, but it seems a very long time away. We all miss you very much. I hope your work is proceeding favourably and that the mine is as good a prospect as the Company hopes. There is much talk on the Ship of mining, as many passengers are travelling to Victoria in the hopes of finding gold; I can't help feeling assured that you are working for a Company and are not Prospeckting in the wild.

Your loving wife, Jacqueline

O, the ache of the nib scratching the white paper. I make myself up, every day I make myself up. I smile and smile and smile. Perhaps I should throw myself in the sea and make an end of this, this tedium.

My daughters trap me in a womanly furrow. Their births so lovely, when they're all suck and ravenous touch, tiny scraps of flesh clinging like carnivorous flowers, so helpless and entirely mine - How sad that they grow and turn their thoughts into secrets, they have sorrows they no longer tell me. Sometimes they're so far away, I feel afraid. What will I do then?

I am yet young. Where my husband is weak, I am all endurance, my children shall look up and see a mountain. And yet he calls me soft and spoilt, he mocks my small hands. It is not just of him. And I am silent, I say nothing, to say the truth would kill him, is that not right? And I am strong enough. What other can I be?

If there's any comfort, it is cold as my heart is. Once I was warm, I knew no better, I spent my warmth and now I'm bitter, bitter, bitter. But I'll not think on that. If I smile and weave the morning together with my hands, all will be well.

These unquiet thoughts, running round and round like a hamster in a mill. The lamp swinging right left right left, I feel I'll go mad, but I cannot, I can't. What am I doing here? Last night I dreamt my wedding, awake gasping with the weight on my chest again, his mother with her looking and the bodice so tight I could scream. That ugly dress. Maybe if I'd borne a son, she'd have forgiven me something of myself.

When I was a child, I was so happy. How often kneeling by the gilded altar I saw through the milky face of Mary a threshold, glimmering with dew - and now the door has opened on a dingy room and I staring through the dark - smaller and smaller and smaller -

Once I breathed and the world breathed with me, I knew no better. When he smiled at me my heart was light, he was a good man, I knew, he loved me, I knew. *You have faith in me*, he said, *it makes me strong*. And my heart swelled with pride, that I could be the earth on which he stood. I married him for that. As soon as he was sure of me, that I was his like a lap dog, like a prize brood mare, he brought out the whip of his indifference. I didn't know what poisons he would plough into me, I didn't know what gashes he would carve into my heart, I didn't know how soil leaches, whitening with exhaustion, poorer and poorer, until at last the trees stand stark and naked on a naked hill.

When I was virgin and whole the sea was different, it was a horse and I was fearless. I was blown out across its expanse without harm, I knew too little to care who I was. Now I am small and timorous, a nose poking out from the wainscot, a scurry of frills, a noise of yes. I put my hand to the ladle and the crib and arrange the silver. How is it I despise myself so much?

How lovely the new moon over the water.

It is like the hunt, early, when the mist curls low about fetlocks and the pheasants startle from hedges and the horse shies and riding the shy without effort. And muscle bunching for the leap headlong into who knows what with nothing but the sudden endless wind and the speed...

Mr Haricot, yes, and Mr James, they look on me with such veiled eyes, a shiver of pleasure, yes, to know that still I can make them look, but deeply, safely, secretly, I'll not let them know that I know, I am remote and polite, I am a wife, taken, labelled, it is safer that way. That gypsy woman on the dock, she made me flinch, I did not want to see inside her face, so wild, so indifferent, but she looked at me like a man might look, I did not know where to put my eyes, even in all that bustle of trunks and farewells and handkerchiefs, she standing there with an armful of fish, hard and stern and dark, her breast all full and shadowed and a barelimbed child clinging at her skirt, and yet, I could not turn away, not for that second, she accused me, she claimed me, she with all her filth and wanton smile, her old dress and bold earrings, unhusbanded, her brightness and her dark, the smell of her as if she'd been with men, that look, I cannot rid myself of thinking of her, before the crowd closed up and she vanished and the ship took me away.

The children who I love but yet they tire me, they eat me up, they leave nothing over. When my husband pulled them on his knee and tickled them I'd want to kill them, running over with their gifts for a smile given without pain, without travail, and he so casually Lord. I'd kill them for the pleasure of his shock, maybe then he'd know at last, maybe then his face would open up and let out all the blood I've given for him, maybe then he'd see the prison that he is. But how can I think that, how can I think, my mind's not right.

They'll grow and grow and turn on me their beauty, then I'll be old and worn and empty.

Who am I when I'm not a wife?

How lovely the moon upon the water.

III Analects

Years ago, I started a story that I never finished with the words: *My grandmother spoke five languages and lied in all of them.* We inherited the myths in which my mother robed herself, the legends of a glorious, lost past, of her parents' wedding at Winchester Cathedral, of distinguished and bemedalled ancestors, of a family that *belonged*, not only to each other, but in a place and time and society. For years she treasured these fragments to protect herself against exile and wrapped us lovingly inside them, ensuring perversely that we would never belong anywhere. And beneath these luminous myths we sensed other rumours, idly flapping like black leaves through gutters of conjecture, heralds of a twisted, poisonous vegetation that always grew there.

At thirty three, I rummage through the few artefacts we possess to tell us of our history. There are some photographs: a portly man in full dress uniform, braids, sword and plumed helmet, who seems to be short: his head is tilted back and he is looking down his nose through a pair of wire-rimmed spectacles. He is Sir Charles Stevens, my great great grandfather, at one time Governor-General of Bengal, who studied at Melbourne University in 1860, and was the occasion of an editorial in *The Times* when he returned to Britain and beat all the Oxford graduates in their final exams. Who was he? And there is the gold-rimmed miniature of Lady Duff-Stevens, my great grandmother, an attractive, firm-chinned woman of about thirty with an expanse of white throat on which gleams each tiny, individually painted pearl. Some kind of scandal aureoles her, tales of an affair, a divorce... There is the angelic boy who was the model for the Pears Soap advertisement, a cousin of my grandmother who later became an Admiral (and whose nickname in the service, inevitably, was Bubbles). There was my great great grandmother, who hailed from an aristocratic Italian family and who would imperiously demand of my trembling grandmother, when she was a girl - *Child? Do you like men?* And when my grandmother whispered - *Yes, Granny,* she would laugh and say - *Good! So do I!* Or some other cousin of my grandmother, who lived among the monks in Tibet and whose greatest treasure was a necklace made of human veterbrae, given to him as a token of the highest honour, which he kept in his modest flat in the south of England where he wrote his memoirs. There is the legend of the letter sent to my grandmother by Uncle Bee, at that time the Governor-General of India, in which he told her that he was going to kill himself, which he did (official reports said it was an accidental overdose)...

I could go on sorting through these tatters, looking for something like an explanation. They offer an ambiguous inheritance: a possibility of honour, a possibility of choosing absurdity, humiliation, folly, death, over the compromise of some essential kernel of self: these sad, complex people whose inflexible wills hammered them down to the bedrock of tragedy. What am I to do with these ghosts who claim me, whose bloodstained heritage has given me the remnants of a privilege that is as disabling and dangerous as innocence? How do I speak to them?

I liked visiting my grandparents. At first they lived in a two-storey cottage and we would sleep in the attic. It had sloping ceilings with windows let into them and cream-yellow wallpaper with a fine floral diagonal print. At the back of the house there must have been stables, for I remember horses and the clop of hooves over cobblestones and a huge wooden mounting block from which Grandpa hoisted me into the saddle.

When we were there, my grandparents would bring out the books their own children had read: beautiful hard-covered books with paper you knew was old because of its yellowing fragility, with intricate ink-lined illustrations painted in with watercolours. Or the puzzle blocks, worn at the edges, which were kept in cardboard boxes fragile with age.

Granny's hair was long and, even then, pure white. She seemed to personify an exquisite femininity; her soft white presence expressed a distance and gentleness which seemed at once evanescent and immeasurably strong. I loved watching her brush the long white fall of her hair with the special silver-backed brush with its soft yellowing bristles, and looking at her dressing table with its little pots and perfume squirters which contained the particular smell of her. She smelt as if her skin were talcum powder. I would watch in fascination as she twisted the hair and fixed it in a hairnet with the hairpins that were always scattered about the table into the neat, precise bun she always wore on the back of her head. She worked in a dress shop in Falmouth and once I visited it, awed by the elegantly plain glass window with its single displayed dress and the controlled efficiency of the staff. We went upstairs and watched the seamstresses cutting out the cloth and sewing it together, inhaling the smell of freshly cut wool and cotton and the faint scent ("*scent*, not *perfume*," my grandmother would tell us) which hung so alluringly around them. A long time ago, before I was born, she had worked at Elizabeth Arden in Paris: and once she had been the sixteen year old heiress whom my grandfather had married and whom he remembered to us with desire still palpable in his voice.

Grandpa smelt fragrantly of tobacco and he spoke with the precise vowels which later we were taught, against our will, in Australia. He still wore the bearing of his army service and he was moustached and bald, with a large, sensual nose. Sometimes he came to stay at our house and once the leg of his bed went right through the floorboards, an occurrence which seemed miraculous, as if he were Rumpelstiltskin. I don't remember Granny staying. We were not allowed to wake him up and our impatience made the privation endless. After he had gone home, I would run to the spare bedroom in the morning with the hope that he was still there and was sharply disappointed when I found the bed empty, even though I really knew, but I had imagined it so clearly that I was almost convinced that I had summoned him, as if I imagined hard enough the world would magically reform into the shape of my wishing. When I was about ten, at the time my father's father died, I dreamt that Grandpa was dead: and I woke with an intolerable feeling of desolation. I loved him in a way I was unable to love my father, although I didn't know that then. His pride, when he walked with his three granddaughters, illuminated the air for us: my mother was his only daughter, and we were his favourite grandchildren, a favouritism which intensified later when we moved to the other side of the world and caused, although we didn't know it, implacable resentment among our cousins. My memories of Grandpa are much less discrete than those of Granny, who was always enclosed in distance: he played with us and drew us inky pictures of elephants and circuses and little men with big ears, and took us for walks along the beach where we would listen for the ice cream van and run to be bought a vanilla block of ice cream wrapped in foil paper. Or he would tell us stories of India, where he was born, of the cobra that crawled into his cot when he was a baby or rhymes of Rudyard Kipling, or he would spin us the miracle of the birth of my mother, when he was so excited he had to have another brandy while he walked up and down outside the bedroom where my grandmother was in labour.

I remember another house, not nearly so well: this had only one storey and a garage at the side where Grandpa kept rows and rows of hamsters, one of which he gave to me. Hamsters were not satisfactory pets. They slept all day and if you picked them up they bit your finger, splattering blood everywhere. The second house, which had a garden, gave way to a flat. I remember visiting that once, in an atmosphere of restraint or discomfort, and admiring the little plaster plate I had given on a previous visit, now carefully placed on the mantelpiece. When I think of this time, I have an abstract vision of my grandparents fleeing desperately from debts, retreating to places where they were more and more invisible, until they came to the council flat in Falmouth where they lived for the next twenty years and where finally Grandpa died.

From my mother's childhood I can only collect rumours and the silences surrounding them, glimpses on a tide continually withdrawing into darkness. She sometimes speaks about the War.

My father used to laugh at her squeamishness when she refused to watch war films. She could never bear violence, it called up too much within her. Her own violence had the terrifying neutrality of a natural element. She was a small child during Hitler's blitzes of Britain: there are tales of hurried evacuations, of crouching for hours in the dark of bomb shelters while her father told her funny stories, of three family houses bombed, of Uncle Tiny, who died in the sinking of *HMS Hood*, and who is the relative whom I most resemble. I remember looking at my grandmother's sepia photograph of him, eighteen years old in smart naval uniform, and recognising my male face.

I have sometimes wondered how much the war still exists within our family, whether the pain and silences which seem so much part of our legacy, which we have struggled so hard to overcome and which are still defeating us, are shadows of the war. But which war? The deadly, interminable wars between men and women, between possibility and its betrayal, between children and their parents, the colonists and the colonised, between the past and the present, memory and forgetting: all these are seeded in the shadows of a barely decipherable history. The war between my parents was no different.

My family, my mother says, bisecting the world between *them* and *us*: but ours was a displaced invention of specialness, a specialness which divided even the nuclear fragment that was our family in Australia. C, for instance, was excluded from the imprimatur: she was *like a Croggon*, although in many ways she was perhaps most like our mother, as in many ways I was most like my father.

My parents' marriage might be seen as the tragedy of two people who never learnt how to speak to each other, perhaps because they assumed that it was possible. And if I saw poetic language as a means of escape from the dull purgatory in which I lived as a child, it was also an attempt to bridge the gulf between the realities I experienced and what I was told to believe about them; perversely, a struggle to find truth. Language in our family was a protective covering to ward off truth: one was never to say how things actually *were*. To do so was an embarrassing breach of given reality. Perhaps, through poetry, language could be made that fitted the world as I knew it, both the acknowledged and unacknowledged realities, instead of leaving a gap through which I fell, again and again, into an abyss of meaninglessness. I'm not sure I have outgrown this desire, despite its impossibility: and perhaps, if one wishes to write poetry, one never should.

As children in Australia, we were alone, as alone as any Chinese or Greek family would have been in a small Victorian country town, despite the fact that, like our neighbours and schoolfriends, we spoke English. We had no cousins, grandparents, aunts or uncles to cushion us from our difference. Our accents branded us as foreign, but deeper than that, it was a construction of mind, an unconscious inheritance of privilege which persisted despite our dirty, undarned uniforms and unbrushed hair full of grass seeds, and which people sensed and, mostly, resented. If it was also the defensive privilege adopted by the persecuted, it smelt no less sour. I was perfect fodder for classroom bullies: unattractively shy, bespectacled, plain, clever and completely unable to defend myself: worse, I was full of the painful pretensions of a child who had decided that she was going to be a great poet. Adults didn't warm to me: I was too inturned, too graceless, perhaps too arrogant. This didn't apply so much to my sisters, who were more nimble at scaling the intricate systems of social status than I was.

My father was seldom there. He was working at the mine, a china clay pit being set up near Ballarat. He was sacked in dubious circumstances and for a while sold aluminium cladding, a job for which he was spectacularly unsuited. He gave that up when, after spending an evening persuading an old couple to buy the cladding they evidently couldn't afford, he spent the rest of the night persuading them they didn't need it. Then he worked for the Mines Department in Melbourne. By then my parents' marriage was probably unsalvageable. He lived in Melbourne, returning to our small farm on alternate weekends. His presence sparked the nightly, interminable fighting, to which, unable to sleep, I would always listen, crouched behind the kitchen door. I could never hear what my father said: his voice was a low rumble underneath the loud anger of my mother, with her endless accusations punctuated by violence. We had a dozen clay mugs which were always in pieces from being thrown at my father and which I remember him patiently reglueing with Araldite.

The conflicts in my parents' marriage were as much about class as sex and money. My father hated and feared the stigmata of my mother's class, which she bore indelibly, without consciousness of their presence. My mother was beautiful, although she was no coquette, and in a sense - although she understood she was beautiful - was unaware of its potency, and of the pain it caused my father by its mere presence. Her beauty, more than anything else, made him afraid and angry, as if he had no right to it. Or so I suspect. My father was brutal to my mother in ways he never perhaps understood, or hid from himself. He was a secret country, full of intricate webs of deception, a man who could keep knowledge secret from himself to an extent I am unable completely to understand. Appearance, because he was so unsure of what was inside him, was everything to him, and my mother, who did not care about how things looked or what other people thought, threatened to tear apart his carefully maintained fiction of himself with her anarchic honesty. He was careful never to let her succeed, and when she did, when at last, to his disbelief, she left him, it was too late for both of them.

Their conflicts were played out in money. My mother never knew how much my father earned: her sins were to be expiated through work. He gave her a tiny weekly allowance with which she had to buy clothes, shoes, food for all the animals, including children, and any other supplies for the household and farm. She made do by making our bread, raising poddy calves for beef, and keeping a cow for milk, butter and cheese and chickens for eggs. My father refused to buy a new washing machine, although ours was ancient and even had a mangle. This lasted until my mother left and he had to do the washing. Everything we had was second-hand. I was thirty before I bought a set of new saucepans, from sheer lack of practice.

My father's brutalities were seldom expressed in physical action. He never smacked any of us. My mother's discipline, in line with her practice of horse training, was firm, rational and corporeal. I spent a large part of my childhood terrified of her anger. No doubt my father was equally terrified, although that didn't occur to us as a possibility: nevertheless, I think all of us were aware of his fragilities and grew up with a desire to protect him, as my mother did, from the knowledge of his own weaknesses.

We wanted to make our mother happy, but we never could. She'd weep and silently we'd try to comfort her, stiff and embarrassed, or her anger would flare out of some misdeed, objects which were lost or some task undone. Somehow it was our fault. *I should never have married your father*, she'd tell us, and our existences vanished: we were mistakes, derailments of fate, which should have been for her a grand country house and luxurious stables full of polished horses and a husband who adored her and children who were good and kind, like we weren't, except possibly F.

I constructed a world, like most lonely children, in which I was superior to everyone else, despite all appearances to the contrary. If my day to day reality was one of mundane depression and low-level persecution, this served to confirm my fantasy of privilege. For aren't all geniuses persecuted by an ignorant world? And since my sisters were so much more socially successful than I was, I adopted a role of literary sage. C remembers still, with the sting undiminished, the time when I told her, officiously, that she was incapable of writing good poems.

I armoured myself quite consciously with fantasy. My private realities became those of the kind of poetry I found in the school readers I would pick up in jumble sales: the sonorous seductions of John Masefield and Alfred Noyes, the romantic dislocations of Adam Lindsay Gordon, the intricate beauties of Alfred Lord Tennyson: although, since I read everything in our library - I was always hungry for books - my magpie reading also embraced T.S. Eliot, William Blake, Wallace Stevens, e.e. cummings, D.H. Lawrence and William Wordsworth, whose *Prelude* lived for a time in our toilet, the only private room in the house. I admired them all indiscriminately. My imagination was nourished by the natural world: moonrise over the dam, lying in foot-high grass watching the sky, the nightly splendour of sunset: most especially when, early in the autumn mornings, I would run out to see the unblemished sky shading through translucent pinks and mauves to a deep transcendent blue - the blue which da Vinci painted in his *Madonna of the Rocks* - against the tangled silhouette of the oak trees, through which shone a single vagrant star. These always spoke to me of somewhere else: when some natural wonder caught my breath I would always imagine it as a reflection of another, fabulous place, where magic was real. Or that it was England, which was far enough away to be the same thing. These displacements were nevertheless underpinned by a country child's practical acceptance of phenomena like birth, shit, hard work and death. When, at ten, I read *The Lord of the Rings*, I found my religion: because the book was unambiguously fantastic, it satisfied my desire for escape from a life which I could only endure with a kind of stoic grimness, while at the same time it did not compromise what I knew to be reality, as an authentic religion might have done, by forcing me to examine myself, something I fervently didn't wish to do. I had already decided what reality was: it was deeply disappointing and completely godless. I was intellectually elitist about fantasy: a major reason Tolkien captivated me was the scale of order of his 'secondary reality', its moral structure and in particular its etymology: although even then I recognised that Coleridge's *Kubla Khan* was a masterpiece which Tolkien could never hope to rival. I have often regretted that I didn't throw my pubescent enthusiasm into a study of ancient Greek or Middle English, which would have been ultimately more useful to me, but this was partly ignorance and, perhaps, a kind of cowardice. For all his love of books, my father was suspicious of writing. It was not, he felt, quite legitimate as a pursuit: and although I studied and loved Latin for four years, I was advised to give it up and study maths and sciences, because they would be more useful towards a career. I failed them spectacularly, to the chagrin of my teachers. Perhaps failure was the only act of rebellion open to me.

It is increasingly clear to me that the border between memory and imagination does not exist in any definitive sense, but shifts, an expanding and contracting twilight. The past is as mysterious as the future: we never really know what happened there. The unmediated recollections I have of England, between the ages of four and seven, are motionless, undramatic and strangely unpopulated: other people existed as facts in my cosmos, rather than as the levers of events. When I was old enough, I began to construct my own narratives of reality, but I have no way of knowing how close the notations here are to those I constructed then. All this remembering exists in the present.

All language is fiction, which is not to say it is a lie. But behind and before language, beyond its polarities and contradictions, exists the shimmering expanse of what is. And it is desolating to discover, as we approach the margins of presence, that what appears to be manifest is as unstable as words are, that everything we can understand is shaped by our sensual perceptions, that not even matter can be absolute. No wonder we return, with empty hands, to language, for it is the only place where truth exists. We already know the dilemma of words, their deceptiveness, their glamour, but perhaps within them still exists a centre where a meaning might yield itself to our seeking bodies. Like an optometrist continually shifting lenses in front of a staring eye, I am looking for a form through which I can refract, however fleetingly, a clarity. And this is so riddled with uncertainty: my instruments are too crude, my sightings unverifiable, my destination unknown, and truth a horizon continuously receding before me...

IV Adelaida

I knew what it meant then but now I don't know if I am sad or happy or nothing at all. It's like the little mermaid who lost her tongue and walked with knives in her feet and when she died the clouds lifted her off the waves like spume and wove her among the sunbeams until she wasn't there at all. If I hold my eyes half shut the light shatters on my lashes, maybe it is like that, and the breathing of the ship is really my chest creaking with the labour of holding myself here. The sails crack loudly as if they're woven out of stone, they belly out, they are not white but the palest of yellows. They are not like flowers, they are like a church. Maybe I'm frightened but if I don't make any noise no one can touch me. I'm safe here inside my skull, looking out. The floor isn't a proper floor because it moves and underneath it swim all the little fishes and scaly monsters, they'll swim underneath my bed when I sleep at night and look through the dark with their cold pale eyes and call my name. I'll listen for them in the dark, perhaps they'll hear me thinking and press their mouths against the belly of the ship and tell me stories no one has heard before, about the barnacle geese barking in the still nights as they hatch on the rocks and the white seals playing on the ice and fish that fly and the whales sieving the whole sea through their mouths. I can't see anything except the waves, they're so dark, they break white against the planks of the ship and little birds of spray fly up and hurt my eyes. Perhaps I'm crying but I don't cry any more. A whole sea, I never knew I was that big. The others are going into the ship now and the men are shouting. I'd like to take my shoes off like the sailors and climb to the top where the wind stands my hair up like a brush and pulls back their lips over their teeth, like monkeys at the zoo. I'd like to have pictures on my arms to remind me who I am and to knot a cloth around my neck and to walk on the branches like a bird does. Maybe I could touch the sun up there, it might feel like an apple, a silver apple or an apple of glass. I'd look inside and know what a day is, maybe I could put it in a box and keep it there and all the kings and queens of the world would come and beg me to put it back. But I wouldn't until they told me what my name is and then I'd put the name in a box so I'd know where it was. Everything is in a box and the boxes are on the ship but I don't know where. I don't want to go into the cabin, the door looks like a mouth and the steps have no back, I could fall through them and down. If I hold very tight I won't breathe so hard. I don't like the lamps, they're moving and the walls move, the seagirls are pressing their arms against them, they want to come in and take the boxes to their caves so they can open the pianos and swim through the rungs of chairs and let loose the tablecloths and sheets into the shapes of the water. They want all my dreams, I can hear them whispering already. They saw me through the curtains which flinched back before I saw them, they want my princess doll and my books, but they can't break the planks, the planks are too strong, like the men are, brown and polished and smelling like salt and weeds. They'll have to go away and hide in their forests of kelp. I don't want them any more. When the light goes out it is so dark the sea becomes a wind in a forest, the trees walk creaking all night and fly away with the owls. I can't tell if I'm asleep, the colours come and whirl inside my eyes and I hear the witch tapping in my ears. Mamma dreams so many things, she opens the chest at the foot of the bunk and the lamp spills its yellow light across the carved flowers, she opens it and all the dreams unfold, they are tapestries you can walk into. They are birds in green trees with crowns of red berries and the sun flaming across the sky, each flame a golden leaf, a red leaf, a leaf of orange, and all the birds are wingless and beneath them on the grass are lions and foxes and a unicorn with flowers braided through his mane. Or sometimes it is night and pools of lilies reach out to the moon, who is hiding in a white dress. Mamma wears a string of pearls and all the blood flowers from her neck, the sky is the colours of midnight, she is sad and folds her hands against her breasts, they are sad there like doves. I want to hold her but they are only pictures, they melt in my hands and the box closes. Sometimes she is asleep and a little bubble of spit slides from her mouth and down her chin and she mumbles but I can't hear what she is saying. I would like to put my face between her breasts and smell the lace, it's so pretty like foam on the sea, and press her skin to my face, it smells like almonds and milk, but I'm too old. I would like to press my forehead against her belly and feel the sea there. Her feet are little like mine and her hands are strong and brown, like the sailors', but little, and there is a dent where the gold presses in on her finger. Sometimes she looks so old, like the pages of an old book, where the tissue is so soft and crisp over the picture on the shiny paper, and you fold it back and it is like an eye opening. I would like to fold back her hair, but she might wake up, she might ask me who I am. I'd say, I am a vizier's daughter on a magic carpet. I'd say, I am a snowdrop growing in the deeps of the waves. I'd say, I am a pearl hidden in a nutshell in the deepest pool of an ancient forest. She'd look and look, but I wouldn't be there, like I look and look and she *is* there, but I know she isn't there, I know she isn't there at all. Mamma's dressed again and the chest is open and my clothes lie across the bed, empty and waiting for me. It is so cold and the water never stops. I don't want to wear any shoes, Mamma pulls the hair so tight back from my head that I'll tear my skin to frown. I can't breathe. She looks far away and hard. Everything is too small. It smells like fat and sleep and sick and all the blankets look so tired. Why are they so tired Mamma? Maybe they soaked up too many dreams. When I wake up, I'll be old and someone else will have to tell me what I did. I remember a dream I had a long time ago, Papa sitting so straight and silent, he didn't like us, he'd rap the table with his hand and all of us would listen. I thought he was like Zeus on Mount Olympus, his beard all criss-crossed with candlelight, and you nodded Mamma, and all of us so straight, even Fanny. I was little then and sometimes he'd take me on his knee, and there were other times when I knew and then I was so empty, I knew his hand was impatient and the pool of grace soon growing dull and dry. I'd like to be a man with a gun or a sailor climbing up the clouds or the captain coming down from the bridge with a cool face. I'd spit green spots into the ocean and laugh when the ropes cut my hands. I'd walk with my hands behind my back and nod and I'd never wipe the sick off the floor. The sails are angry today, there are shadows running up and down, it's like they're going to shout. The chickens stick their heads out and squawk, their combs flop down over their eyes like they're bleeding, the sea is purpling up with blots of dark like footprints, who is walking there that I can't see? The seagirls are trying to break in, they're sobbing, their hair is all tangled up in the water. What is it they want so much? Their lips are greeny-blue and their eyes are green and when they cut themselves they bleed salt. Their skin is white like the inside of my arm. I wish I knew their names, but it's too loud, they're beating on the planks, and the sharks will come and steal everything and gulp it down behind their shiny rows of teeth. Sharks never sing or cry. Fanny's looking pink and yellow-green, soon she'll be sick, yes, and Mamma lets her play with the necklace that we must never touch. I wish I was sick but I'm never sick. I'd like to have a marlin-pike and hit her so hard there'd be nothing left over inside me and then I'd fly up to the highest spar and call down all the stars, do re mi fa so la ti do, and my hands full of sharp cold edges, I'd hold them gently like baby birds and maybe they'd teach me all the letters of the sky and I could sit all night in the crow's nest, reading. My voice would shimmer like a bellnote and all the creatures of the sea would hear me as if I was a star and follow on the waves, seals and octopus and tunny and whales and mackerel, and the rays would spill from my hands along their backs, and Catherine and Fanny would fall into the waves tumbling over and over and I'd watch them twinkling all the way down to the seacaves until they were sorry. Mamma's eyes are hurting me, if I'm small and quiet nothing will happen. One day I'll go in a ship all by myself with sails all the colours of the rainbow until I find a place where no one has ever been before. And I'll tell them a story that's so far away they've never heard it, and they'll listen to me, all of them will listen, sitting around me in a circle with the light travelling through all their faces, the light inside me that won't come out now. I'll say: Once upon a time a little baby was born. On the first day the little boy was very small and on the second day he was a little bigger and on the third day he stood up in the sky and at last all the people understood. He was born in a stable and the wise men knew, because an angel told them, and the shepherds came running with their sheep and the oxen bowed low. It was small like here and the wind was the wings of angels coming down from heaven to see him, there were so many the trees bent over and the river was pushed out of its bed in a big wave. But the little boy was fast asleep and he had a dream. He dreamed of a big ship sailing through the black clouds and he thought the wings of angels were a storm and every time the oxen stamped the stable shook and he thought it was a wave crashing on the ship. He was very still and very beautiful and his Mamma held him to her bosom and he dreamt she was the sea, blue with the stars shining through her veil like eyes.

V Abidings

My father remains an enigma. I know almost nothing of his childhood, although I have been in its environs: I know the shadows in the house he grew up in, its smell of wellington boots and dogs and floor polish, I know the colours of its flowers and the height of the hedges he hid behind, I know the mud he rolled in as a child and the urinous tanning pits into which he must have stared, as uneasily stirred as I was by their awful opacity. But I don't know who he was, what he thought, what frightened him or made him happy, I don't know what he imagined or dreamed, when he was a little boy growing up in Grampound.

Grampound is a small stony village on the road which runs between St Austell, where we lived on the coast, and Truro, the main town of Cornwall. Its main feature is the tannery, which has been owned by the Croggons for the past three hundred years, although now we hear rumours from England that finally the business is dying. Oak bark tanning is time-consuming and expensive, and makes thick black leather, ideal for saddlery and boots. It is used for the boots of the guards at Buckingham Palace, as I remember being noted on a postcard we bought in London when I was six years old. "The Guard," said the fine print, "is wearing boots made of Croggon leather": and I felt inordinately proud to be a Croggon and to be so intimately linked to royalty. Croggon leather was also used to build the leather boat which re-enacted the legendary voyage of St Brendan across the North Sea to America. Waterproofed with sheep fat, the ship weathered the journey through the ice-floes because of its extraordinary flexibility, which allowed it to breathe like a whale.

The Croggon family house fronts on to the main street of Grampound and is called The Hollies. The frontage, when I saw it last, was white pebble dash: there was a brass door knocker and a letterbox with the basket inside the front door, through which mail arrived twice a day. On the left was the dining room, into which you had to step down. It contained a long polished table and a large carved sideboard, in which was kept the cutlery. Toast racks, salt cellars and so on were kept in curious little cupboards let into the stone wall on the other side. If you sat, as my grandmother Ma did, at the head of the table with your back to the kitchen, you'd face the window, set into the two-foot thick wall, with the seat underneath it, and could see the legs of people walking past.

Behind you, two steps up led to the kitchen, a long room flagged with stone. To the right was a pantry, and next to that a narrow scullery with a sink below a window which overlooked the back garden. The kitchen continued past these rooms: at the far end was a cast-iron wood stove, with enamel lids that were let down over the hot plates. Beside it was a black coal scuttle and poker and in front of it was a small rug where the dogs slept. To the side, under another window at right angles to the one looking out of the scullery, was a pine table scrubbed almost to whiteness. On this table Ma made, every Thursday, pasties which she would sell at the market. Along the opposite wall was a settle, and above that a host of copper warming pans and saucepans with cast iron handles. I conflate the kitchen with a memory of a cartoon-style book I remember looking at one day at The Hollies, on *How To Be a Good Housekeeper*, with step-by-step recipes for macaroni cheese and other cheap dishes and *Making the Most of your Roast*. Ma still kept the habits of frugality she had learnt during the Depression and after the War: every container was emptied until not a drop or a crumb or grain or scrape remained inside it.

In the corner, a dark, narrow staircase twisted upstairs to a landing, from which a few steps led up to the little door of the attic. The attic was full of secrets and forgotten treasures from older childhoods than ours. There were shaving mirrors and tiny little wooden chests of drawers, in which each drawer held glass-covered collections of butterflies. There were trunks full of old clothes, dating back I guess to Edwardian times, and music boxes and a table game of soccer with rods to make the players kick. Whenever we visited The Hollies, we couldn't wait to rush upstairs into that long, twilit room, where the past was kept for us with its distinctive ghostly smell of dust and mothballs and furniture polish. But it is a past that no longer exists: C told me that all the games and mirrors and cupboards have been sold, and now the attic is empty.

Ma's bedroom was upstairs. She slept in a curtained fourposter bed with a carved seaman's chest at its foot. Her dressing table had a glass top, under which were old photographs: I remember only one, of Ma as a young woman, spare, agile and mannish, with a white streak already through her dark hair, just where my own hair is beginning to whiten. Set into the wall was a cupboard with a glass door and sometimes we were allowed to look at the objects inside: intricately carved ivory spheres, containing other spheres, and delicate enamelled boxes and jade figurines. Once, from this cupboard, Ma gave us a detailed plaster nativity set, with a tiny wooden crib in which was glued the infant Jesus. Although later we lost the baby and would set it up each Christmas, Christless.

The Hollies was full of clocks, which my Uncle John wound once a week. He refused to synchronise them and so for five minutes before and after the hour the whole house quivered with chimes.

So far I've been possessed by the desire to see, but I should articulate what I mean by seeing. Sight for me is a problematic sense. Since I came to Australia, I have been extremely short sighted: I can't read the top letter on the optometrist's chart and objects begin to blur at a distance six inches from my nose. I suspect I was not shortsighted before then. Certainly I can remember reading the blackboard at school in England, which was impossible when I came to Australia. When, at about eight years old, I was given glasses, it was a revelation: I had been existing in a world without perspective or distinct form in which

I identified objects and people by colour, movement and sound. From an early age, I was conscious of different modes of sight.

More recently I have noticed that my sight is remarkably variable and that these variations can be linked to my state of emotional being. On bad days I can hardly see at all: I cannot focus clearly and have little sense of perspective. My apprehension of colours is also affected, as if a grey mist hung over my eyes. My mind is turned inwards, obsessively rehearsing one or other of a number of circular dialogues. I have little sense of relation to the world around me. There are other days when I see more clearly, even very clearly, although colours have a faded quality and again I have no sense of connection with what I am seeing. It appears to me as a flat image, without perspective: I am conscious of my sight only as a phenomenon of light on my retina. On good days, I am acutely conscious of colours and forms and movements. Mostly I am aware, then, of sight as a dimension of touch: that the light which touches me also touches everything I see. At these times, I can become a whole landscape. The self is no longer a mendacious trap but a channel through which all passes, transforming and transformed. Everything is plump, rounded, gravid with its potential. Objects seem to hold within them a sense of immanent life: and living beings, no matter who or what they are, contain a luminosity, yet hidden, which trembles beneath their surfaces as if, shortly, a cloud would break and reveal the divinity of the sun.

I have one memory of The Hollies which I seem to inhabit: a Christmas when the sitting room was full of people and talk. The room was a cornucopia of curious objects which Grandpa had brought back from Saudi Arabia after the War: a brass elephant full of foreign coins, some with holes, some hexagonal, which we could spread out and count on the carpet, other elephants carved of ebony and ivory, and short, curved daggers with carved handles and flowers etched into the blade. The tea trolley would come into the sitting room at four o'clock every day, brought by the woman (Madge? Maureen? Maude?) who helped in the house. It bore either high tea, chocolate cake and mustard and cress sandwiches, or a plain tea cake and bread and butter. Uncle John's huge arm chair was next to the fire, where with his one arm, aided by the other hard, gloved hand, he would stuff his pipe and light a match and smoke, putting up his feet on tapestried footstools and cushions which Ma had worked in cross-stitch.

That Christmas, we were all three wearing identical dresses: they were red and had white sleeves with hearts on them, or maybe strawberries. I have an image of a tapestried footstool: but mostly I remember my Great Uncle George leaning over the arm of his chair and reciting to me: *There was a boy, his name was Jim, his friends were very good to him...* I listened with a fascinated trepidation, as I was certain he was rebuking me and I didn't know what I had done.

Across the road from The Hollies was the tannery, which consisted of low-roofed open stone sheds separated by narrow stone pathways. They contained the flagged pits of brown-yellow scum-surfaced tannin. Each pit was full of curing hides and the intense organic smell at once made me feel nauseous and quickened my curiosity. The liquid lapped level with the flags and you couldn't see how deep the pits were, they might have gone all the way down to the middle of the earth, nor could you see what was inside them, although you knew it was the skins of dead animals. There was a machine made of knives which stripped the flesh off the hides: my Uncle John had fallen into it when he was a little boy, during the War, and that was why he only had one real arm. There was also a hayshed, with a rope on which, if you had the courage, you could swing out and back, and behind the tanning sheds were fields, where were kept pigs, cows and chickens, and a small pond with ducks and geese. Ma would drive around the village and the farm in her Landrover, a battered army-green vehicle which I think had no doors: certainly I fell out of it one day as she sharply turned a corner and I remember her surprised face looking at me sprawling in the mud, ordering me back into the front seat as if it were my fault I had fallen there.

At the far end of the village off a winding, muddy laneway was Brae Barton, a proper farm run by a huge red-faced man called Rafe. I think the farm was owned by the Croggons, as were many of the houses in the village, including Park Marris, where we lived for a short time after we came back from South Africa. My father and his brothers had spent a lot of time at Brae Barton when they were boys. The heart of the household was the kitchen, one wall of which was taken up by a huge hearth. It had a long pine table and a big settle and the floor was all stone, and there was a black cast-iron boot-scraper by the door. Outside the kitchen was a courtyard and outside that the field, churned into mud by the milch cows. Once or twice we were allowed to watch the milking: the calling cows herded into the milkshed and hitched up to shiny machines, and milk running through the cowdung on the concrete floor. I remember puddles in the mud with reflections of the sky, and a goose that chased me. The warm flank of an animal.

I have very few memories of my grandfather, perhaps because we were children and so had little part in his man's world. The clearest thing I can recall is his sitting on C's bed when she was very ill and giving her a curious necklace, each link of which was an intricately worked silver flower.

In my study is a photograph of him as a young man. He has a handsome, square face with large eyes looking directly at the camera and a clearly defined, sensual mouth. Compared to his other features, his nose is crude, even perhaps a little bulbous. On the back of the photograph is written JOHN RAWSON CROGGON b. 1907. He died of bowel cancer when I was ten, the second time we went back to England.

There were four boys in the family. I remember my Uncle John best: he was a silent man who spoke haltingly and abruptly, as if breaking through to a surface of language was a process of physical struggle. Although he was so taciturn, I was not afraid of his silence. He never married, and lived with Ma at The Hollies. In the huge, immaculately cared-for garden, which was Ma's passion, was a stone outhouse: downstairs was a shed, which smelt of moss and damp and was where Ma plucked chickens. She would string them from the roof and grab handfuls of feathers until the goosepimpled skin was loose and naked, with the stumps of quills still sticking out - you had to be quick and do it while the bird was still hot, or else the feathers would stick in the cold skin. Upstairs was John's room, which we liked to visit. You'd run up stone steps and enter a dark room. At one end was a curtained bed, and underneath a window was an organ with curious markings on the stops, which we would pull and push, treading the bellows which moved heavily beneath our feet as if we were pushing them through water. Here John would paint and read. It was a very private room, although we felt no sense that we were invading it; John was seldom there when we were. His paintings were small oil landscapes with densely textured surfaces of dark mossy greens and sullen greys, with the occasional bright yellow prick of gorse. Once he ordered some green tree frogs for the greenhouse and they magically arrived in the mail, packaged carefully in damp plastic. Once, when we were playing with him, he said in jest: *Don't pull my arm, it'll come off.* But we kept on pulling, and it did. We were all, apparently, horrified. But I don't remember this, I've only been told the story.

The local church in Grampound is Creed Church. Here are buried generations of Croggons. It is, I think, 12th century, very plain and rather small and certainly picturesque, with walls thick enough to have a tunnel through them, behind the pulpit. John would ring the bells at Creed Church with his one arm. I watched him once, breathing shortly in concentration, his arm an instrument of will to send the carillon of chimes floating from the tower over the hushed countryside.

My parents were married at Creed. My mother says she wanted to run away the morning of her wedding, and I have had dreams where I, too, am about to be married, and I am not quite sure why or how, and I am overcome with a paralysing sense of hopeless dread.

Like my mother, my father was a small child during the War. His father was away for a long time and Ma ran the tannery while he was away. When he came back from Saudi Arabia, where he had picked up the local custom of summoning women by clapping his hands, she was directed back into the house. She was a brusque, energetic woman with formidable organisational abilities, and was forced to make do with the Country Women's Association, coffee mornings and jumble sales.

Because of the war, my father was sent away to boarding school in Truro when he was four years old. I don't know what happened to him there. The only memory he has told me from his schooldays is of his literature teacher, a tall man in a black cape who strode between the ranked desks, quoting Keats with such vehement energy that spittle flew from his mouth.

It took until my adulthood to acknowledge how my father lied to me. His lying was a profound omission of truth, a refusal to admit the reality of himself, his desires, his fears, his failures, his love: and its result is an inner emptiness which fills me with a despairing horror. I don't know how to navigate past what he has taught me about truth - that truth does not exist, that trust is impossible, that relationship can only exist through a legislative assertion of authority. How do I dare say to my lover: *you have lied to me*, when my throat closes on a certainty that the lie is, indeed, the case, that it is the whole case, that there is no possibility between men and women of speaking truth? And yet I know it is possible that people might speak the truth to each other. And might this be a possibility that, like the face of God, is imbued with such dread that I dare not even imagine it? I see in my lover's face the same dread. The certainty of lies is much less terrifying than the uncertainty of truth.

Once we walked to a place named Holywell: it was a long journey over sand dunes overgrown with tough grass and there in the dunes, almost completely sunken in the sand, was an ancient chapel, barely recognisable as a building because its walls, perhaps four feet thick, seemed like a formation of the hills. My father had visited Holywell as a boy and our excursion there was in the company of the Croggons. I don't recall much of them except their presence and their serious attention to the sunken chapel. We knelt down and peered through the windows and saw the sand which lifted almost to the roof of its dark abandoned interior.

A little further on was a beach with a cave. Inside the cave, smooth flat ledges of rock stepped up to where water dripped from the ceiling, leaving little stalactites of lime, and ran over the widening ripples of stone until it reached the sandy floor and trickled in a little brook to the sea. I tasted the water: it was refreshing and cold, like no water I had tasted before, as if it had been newly pressed from the heart of rock. This seemed the holier place: it had been shaped by no human hand, although human lips had bent there and slaked their thirst.

VI Ananke

Prithee father, what has thee here? Is't a coin you sold me for melted down to shot? a ploughshare beaten to a sword? a needle unthimbled? slow honey rotted to green poison? - these hands, these hands are too heavy, has aught ever held such weight, I'll rest them on thy head, there. Once so soft, the apples of thy secret mind, the blood inside thy mouth is coal, I'll light it and its air might fan thy lips, and we might talk, thou and I, thou and I -

Why so grim and silent papa? papa? the stones have lips, they spoke once, even they, an earthen thing, a gush of mud. Remember? and the silence and no sign, no, no scrap of red, no rag, all buried, buried, in that cunt of earth - now where did I learn such words, and I so pure a maiden? - in thy ditch papa, where you dragged and buried me. The stones have no lips, only faces, each stone a face, no mouth, no eyes, sneering as they beat me on this bed. They beat me and they tie me and I bite them, father, only for you. I am thy daughter. Don't leave me! - no, stay there. In the stone. We might talk.

Truly, the sky here is godless. A great brutal gong announcing hell. Supplications are useless. The ground a yellow pan and no tree for miles and miles and miles. The hot dark of huts. The women wringing wet in their corsets pouring out a pannikin of water on a dying lettuce: such is the tenderness of womenfolk. The fever in the children, tossing onion-eyed on their truckle beds. The women pouring tea in china cups. How I hate them.

Don't trick me. Thou'rt no bucket for me to piss in, father. I'll empty thee tomorrow in that stinking ditch. They'll loose me and I'll bite them. They shaved my head, I'll go as bald as an old man, the bristle itches, worms crawl from my brain and stand up, affrighted. They bite me in my sleep. I don't sleep: I lie and tell the zodiac of stones: the vixen, the ox, the serpent: the maiden, the goat, the whore: the pannikin, the curlew, the scales: the windmill, the whale, the chapel. I'll tell thy fortune in a trice. They wouldn't hang me, the rope looked at me with loathing. They sent me here to speak with stones, the better to prepare me for my grave. Very grave and considerate is justice, its hammer falls and the world splinters into order.

And you thought me faithless, you thought me slight and fickle, no, my teeth lock even unto death. My curse locked in thy flesh, I turned the key and op'd the door of hell. Or was it heaven? I couldn't tell papa, the angels were infernal, they screamed out of thy wound with red wings. Am I thy bitch? my dugs all barren, whelping mutant puppies in a ditch. You'd have me so, my darling, I'd gnaw thy pate like the bishop in the ice of hell, forever and ever, until you answered me, until the stone split open and spoke its water. Nay, don't wag your head, it is so.

Remember how it was? I remember. I remember and remember in this head as old as Lilith, I am older than that, older than thee, was that what frighted thee? My eyes spoke more eloquent than the axe. I can't forget thee, I can't wash the blood off, it stinks through my dreaming and pours from my hands, there are faces in the puddles every morning, the dark clotted puddles on this stinking floor, they speak to me, they speak to me, but you are silent.

They've confined me in solitude, that's a laugh. They feed me like the bitch you named me, flies breed in my dung, they're pretty, little jewels dancing in the sunlight. I tie them on my private hairs and hang them from my ears, they buzz there, dying. Sometimes I eat them. I eat the lice and fleas, too, when I catch' em, and all the skin rotting off my body. Nothing's safe here, not even me, I am all mouth and hunger. They say you go mad here. I'm not mad, I have conceived a beautiful sanity. Truly, all the tales that ever were are now alive inside me. They keep me from the cold.

They farmed me out, a young lass like me, a pretty maid, you know what happened then, the hot breath, the muddy floor, the filthy cock squeezed inside my mouth, horny fingers shoved inside me, my bleeding arse, all for you papa, all for you, and all the time a poker next my skull yelling *flog her, flog the bitch, flog her to death*, yes, but he was too canny for that, he wanted his piece of white cunt, he wanted his sullen meals and the sour water carried from the river bucket by bucket, he wanted his shoddy hut swept and tidied, yes, I was much too useful. Then one day he went to town and brought me back a bit of lace, *try it on*, he said, *try it on, it's pretty, I got it for you*. I laughed in his face and that night he tied me up and flogged me. I sat on the ceiling and watched my body jumping on the floor, blood from my nose and mouth and ears and cunt and arse, then a red star scorched me and when I woke up he was sobbing, like you papa, sobbing and sobbing, his big clumsy hands all noisy with his tears and snot. *I love you*, he said. He thought I was dead. And truly I was dead, I'd died long before. But I didn't tell him. I didn't speak again ever after that and he got frightened and when the cuts healed he brought me back and traded me. He knew I'd kill him one day.

But you never touched me, did you, papa? never never never never never. Only banished from thy sight. How I hated thee. Thy dead eyes, regarding me from nowhere. Thy dead voice, condemning me. I heard a choir of angels and a scream, they were the same. Dost thou know that yet, in thy wisdom, in the lap of God?

Who named me whore? Was it thee? But none bought me ever, none even touched me, no matter how rich his purse nor how stiff his cock. Still in my centre, the hymen of myself, unbroken. Answer me this riddle, what difference from a cock or a poker? My fingers give me better pleasure. What is a man to me? I hated them all, who fucked me for a bed, or a pallet of hay, or a rum. Them who thought they owned me. Aye, and there's a secret pleasure there, to see their gasping faces, and know myself cold and judging as stone, yes, truly I gave nothing away. There was one - aye, there's always one.

Listen, I'll tell thy fortune. I'll look into this cauldron - stench! yes, a hot beginning and a cold end, twice crowned and a million times dishonoured, but that's the tale of each of us - worms there, but none of them are thriving, and a cold glitter of light. Ah, I see a man on a lonely road, a black ship departing from an empty dock, a dog with many tongues and a red gate - yes, a forest made of flesh, and all the trees weeping and the bandage of thyself unravelling - further, further still, and now I see a hole in the centre of the world, it is thyself, or is't mine? no, I can't tell yet, they are putting out thine eyes and stopping up thy mouth, all the little demons with their pokers, they are branding thee, this will go on forever and ever - now there is a black mist, I see nothing more -

I remember the day I was born, it was raining, it always rained at my birth, slow fat rain and my mother groaning. Who was my mother? I'll tell thee. The sweet water, the first begetter, before there was earth or height or depth or name. I made the worm, the dragon, the cunt-fanged monster, the lion, the mad dog, the man scorpion, the howling storm, and all of them were chained and slaughtered, they pulled their fangs and stamped out their poison, I was nothing left. But I was born again as always, not even death can stop me. Them with their whips scourging the skin off my ribs, them with their rat-hungry factories, them with their rules and goosequills, them with their lips curled up at my stink, none of them can stop me. Not even thee. Eh, papa? what spawned under thy foot? and not until it grew and spat in thy face did you perceive its beauty.

Is't true, you think? Maybe I'm drunk on sorrow, that's a sour glass, rising with a thick head of nightmares. Mayhap I'm mad. 'Twould be a nice physician to find the diagnosis, there's no physicians here, only guards with carmine noses. A bucket and a window with stripes across the morning. The governor came once, a humanitarian, his hands shaking when he left me. My smile unsettled him, he couldn't look right nor left, nor straight ahead, and so examined his boots. Very shiny they were, I'd seen nothing that clean for a lifetime of lifetimes. They blabbed about their master, he scuffed them on the floor but they wouldn't stop their tongues, saying *nice nice nice* and him all pink with holding his breath and trying not to show it. That night I got a soup with no cockroaches and another blanket and a fresh pail of water and some washed clothes. He came next week, talking about education. Education? I said very pretty, m'lud, I've been educated, it never did me no good. I can do a good exegesis on the two thieves, I continued, and once I could translate Virgil into tolerable English, m'lud, but the whips will get thee in the end, and god thundering his gavel above it all, he never had no time for women. I wanted, I told him, to be a priest, and when my sex became evident my heart broke and never mended since. I was a bad girl from then on and not even Jesus himself could save me. But surely, he said kindly, you could do better than this? With your intelligence, and (he said, his nose doing its best not to wrinkle) your tolerable appearance, you might have made a good match. You may yet, he said. I felt badly for him, he wouldn't last long, nor he did, missing the point like an archer with his back turned. This world was made for punishing, not kindnesses. But sometimes I think on him, I never found much kindness.

Aye, there was one. Who was he, papa? We met where things were nameless. In the desert was a rose, it had dew on its eyelids and a thousand thorns. Its roots went down to hell and I climbed them branch by branch, spitting earth from my mouth. There was one, we met in hell. Maybe he's still there, maybe he's dead at last, sleeping in the arms of earth like once he slept in mine, and I looking on the beauty of his face, all the suffering sleaved in sweet repose. They called him a monster, he was monstrous with pain. O my criminal lover! chained as I was, ulcers at his wrists and ankles, and behind us the great forest with its hidden sky. His sweetest cock and strong fine flanks and subtle mouth, such joy I had on him it hurts to think of. He read the mysteries of my body like a bible, he was my dark beautiful continent. But you'll think me sentimental, what is this soggy heart? no, it was wild and free then, no whip could tarnish me. Thy face vanished, yes, he was straight and gentle in my sight. We had our dreams like all lovers until the scowl darkened on the foreman and he sent him off to no man's land. Or did I kill him? No hell compares with that, once knowing heaven. Better to stay blind than to taste the living waters. Better never to speak than once to sing. That was thy creed, papa, thy gob all stuffed with silence. But I'm lying. It was never mine.

Speak! why don't you speak? Sometimes it seemed so close, a breath away, before I murdered thee. An earful of poison, an axe in the garden, a knife in the scullery, a stumble on a high cliff, maybe I just broke thy heart, I forget, the stories mumble themselves all night and in the morning the birds are chirping them, I misremember which is me and which is thee and which is others, all of us are one. Dying takes too long. When was it that I started dying? In the cradle was it or peeping out from mid my mother's thighs or maybe when I quickened in her womb? Was there joy at my making papa or was it truly my first death? O Jesu, I want to die, but that I might linger here, a sad wraith, all nightgowned in mould and ghostly tears running down me, too late, too late. What is't to be alive? to be a candleflame in a storm, condemned to its sorry light, dreaming of chandeliers - I always was provoked by what they call the human condition, I could never cultivate a philosophical resignation -

Aye, the stones have lips, they're telling me - *never never never never never* - what is that word? or is't *ever ever ever ever ever* - I might have thought they'd learn instructions in silence from thee, how is it they're so animate and voluble, I look again and they are dry and stern, like thee, like me. When god died papa I thought the world would never speak again. Father? Did I murder thee? Why dost thou turn so deaf and resolute away? What shall I tell thee? Another story, papa, to while away thy death? Wait, I'll rummage through my head and find one, no, it's all as empty as a sieve to carry water. Mayhap my heart is fuller - but I left it on an island when the ship abducted me, the rats ate it up. Or maybe I am lying and I hid it in the corner under some straw. Even my gut is empty, nothing left to vomit. Nothing left. What of the rose, wincing out of stone and flooding the air with song? such lips are crueller than any warder - they say, *I am the truth, the light and the way*, they say, *love is stronger than death.* They say, *this once is eternal.* Cruel poems writhing out of hell. Even that must wither. Did I kill him, did he murder me? Or are we still locked in our infernal embrace, imagining heaven? Why won't the silence answer? Why don't you answer me?

Who art thou, father? Who are you, papa? A foolish, fond old man... nay, thy silence is my silence, nay, I am the queen of a cerulean heaven, amid the stilly stars - dost thou laugh? Aye, and I laugh also - the most dire certainty is dawn, to us shades - Were you ever as I made you? Did I not legislate thine absence, the better to articulate my realm of solitude? And how shall we find hope here, where all hopes are slaughtered - the bell tolls, *too late, too late*, the stones grin, the rats celebrate after their fashion, the blood speaks - but no, it's not thy blood that falls each morn and leaves me skeletal, nay, none of thee, rose, warder, stone, master, star, neither the poker nor the cock, neither the hand nor the whip, nor the eye, nor the mouth, nor the pen scratching over parchment - none of thee, none of thee -

This dying takes too long, a slow letting, a hard labour. Mayhap you spoke, I didn't hear, the devils bark all night in hell, my skull a kennel of torment. Maybe not. I prophesy you'll never speak, all stopped up in thy tomb, where I hid thee. You'll stay there, it is a proper burial, and I too. All childhood is ghosts, when we reach the length of our graves. I'll imagine me awake and unprison me, stone by stone. Dost thou laugh? Or am I laughing? What is this body I know myself by? Is't mine? Surely not, it was stolen at my birth, I'll find another more particular to me. My breath is a poor bellows but I'll furnace up my heart and forge a new one. Slower and more painful, every breath. I must breathe thee out, each atom of thee, thee out of me, me out of thee, until all stops and the darkness closes over. Then we'll see.

How is't the walls dissolve? And outside them, an unmapped country. Why did I think the forest so unfriendly? Wait! Don't go yet father, we have yet to finish, thou and I. Still thou hast condemned me, answer me that. Answer me that! Nay, only the stones held thee, they are vanishing. These chains that were thy smile, they are vanishing. This poor pallet stinking of thy blood, it is vanishing. That iron bucket, vanishing. How is it I am so afraid? Such trinkets were how I told myself, a bitter rosary, they leave but air and a trace - of what? the fat of sickness boiled down to ambergris? This thin stick, *I*? Who am I?

I'll lie in hell no more. There's truth for a window, a cold air that pains me, the one death I cowered before, and beyond that, nothing that I know. This tired flesh, rotting into earth, and the earth breathing. The perfume of the rose, freed from its secret heart, shaping like a question. My heart is an eagle, rending its talons on its chains. I never heard its cries.

VII Africa

Sometimes it seems to me that I am writing this in order not to go mad. In this limbo which is my life, this writing is the spar which promises, within the clench of my hand, the hope of a ship: or, if no hope, then at least the bare possibility of endurance. I don't wish to speak of my immediate situation: indeed, to do so would be misleading, as the pressures which threaten the fractures I am afraid of exist before now, among these memories and imaginings I am attempting to record. But looking on them is looking on an ice sea, where the sun strikes brightly on the bergs and the water widens darkly between them.

As I write, I tease out a double strand: the imaged memories, available and immediate, which constitute the construction I know as myself, and a shadow strand winding around it, which contains few or no images and is without a language. The other is a series of gaps which becomes apparent as I write down what is visible. There is little sense of discovery in this: I have long been aware of these gaps within myself and have attempted to free myself from their diabolic pressures, so that I might cease a particular process of self destruction that has subtly inhabited and distorted the possibilities of my life. I don't believe it is possible, or even desirable, to heal them: but in the process of discovering what they are, I hope to find a means by which I can live with them.

But how to overcome the torment of hope?

This writing is my present. The struggle is to exist only here, without hope and without despair, in patient endurance: not as a mule hardening its skin against blows, but as a tree which expands joyfully into the storm. I am battling a sense of hopelessness and futility. I don't know how what I write in these pages can possibly matter: I see myself in all my mundanity, unable to reach beyond my own perception. I am seeking in these vagrant and disconnected memories an immanence, an intuition that has fed me throughout the alienation of most of my adult life and which allowed me to construct a faith where none exists. Faith? Writing is nothing else but faith. If one is to speak, one must make oneself up; but who is doing the making up?

Last weekend my oldest son brought out the atlas and I showed him, on the map of Africa, the place where I was born. It doesn't even rate a dot: I know it is about forty miles from Johannesburg, in the Transvaal, and that I lived there until I was four years old, when my parents returned to England with the three of us. As a child I spoke Afrikaans, none of which I remember. It is, like English, a bastard tongue, cobbled out of Dutch and Pidgin English and Xhosa. My father would shout *Footsak!* as he threw stones at stray dogs to chase them off our property, so that is the only word that remains to me: that, and the half mumbled version of *Who Killed Cock Robin?* which C and I both retain, perhaps because its rhythm and trills gave us pleasure when we sang it as children and we were proud, later, of our ability to sing a song in a strange language. That language, hidden in my memory, is another barrier: I cannot speak to my child self. I don't wholly understand her.

My father became a miner because, he said, as a Cornishman he had two choices: farming or mining. He was a younger brother and my uncle Billy was to inherit the tannery which was the family business. He attended the Camborne School of Mines and as a young man travelled to work in Canada with his brother Jeremy. When he returned home he did two years of National Service and courted, in a reportedly lackadaisical fashion, my young mother. There is a photograph of him at the time, looking rather like David Byrne of Talking Heads, an image difficult to reconcile with the man I know now. My parents moved to Carltonville shortly after they were married and all of us were born in that scrubby, raw mining town on the edge of the veldt.

He worked for Western Deep Levels, a gold mine which at that time was the deepest in the world. It took an hour for the men to reach the bottom in the cage, rattling into the bowels of the earth in pitch blackness. The men passed the time by kicking each other with their steel-toed boots. It was so hot my father had to take salt tablets to make up for the sweat he lost, and from thirteen stone he dropped to nine, weight he never regained. The pressure of the stone above the stopes compressed the stout six foot wooden roof supports down to two feet in the space of a twelve hour shift.

It was a place of violent humours and frequent accidents. The stopes were made by blasting and one of the men had a form of shell-shock from the continuous explosions. It meant that he couldn't prevent himself from imitating the hand gestures of anyone standing in front of him. A standard joke was to approach him when his hands were covered with oil and engage him in conversation while rubbing one's hands all over one's face. It made him uncontrollably angry. Another time, my father told me of a fall of razor-sharp rock which sliced open the thigh of one of the men from groin to knee, so a great flap of muscle hung open. Because the man was in shock there was, at first, no blood, so that it was possible to see the patterns of veins and sinews in the muscle. There were five other men on the stope, including my father, and they rushed to bind up the leg, but suddenly all of them, including the injured man, started giggling uncontrollably and couldn't do anything to help. The man almost bled to death.

My father told me once of a curse that was put on the stope which he was managing. The natives were afraid and refused to go in, so he went in himself and removed it. As he picked it up, he felt a sensation like an electric shock and an overwhelming premonition of evil. The object was a ram's horn, stuffed with wool. He took it out as quickly as he could, and threw it away.

... a white wall with a picture on it and through a white veil I see my parents silently backing towards the wall, facing me but receding, and I am seized with a desolation of fear...

...there is a white table in a white kitchen and on the table a glass of milk and I drink it and the milk has turned sour...

...I am asleep in my bed and when I wake up a witch flies out of my ear...

...I sit in the cane bush in the corner of the garden and eat its papery insides and think and think and think but I can't remember being inside my mummy's tummy...

...I am outside with my father and see them, all the stars, flaring like huge jewels thrown across the sky, bright reds and yellows and greens and blues...

...we drive along the road at night and on each side of the road fires are burning...

...we capture a chameleon and put it in a cardboard box and watch its colour infinitesimally ebb from brown to yellow...

...there is a long car ride through the night, with blankets and luggage piled in the back, and all of us sleeping in the eternally humming box...

...there is a ship and the name Durban and looking out of the deck to the receding harbourside and the widening green water...

...and in the water are floating thousands of red jellyfish...

...on the boat a fancy dress party and I win a black doll, beautifully dressed in gold braid, with which I refuse to play...

...we are living at Park Marris in Grampound and I am standing on the crazy paving smelling the bitter scent of alyssum...

...there is a thunderstorm and I wake up and bring my bear to my parents' bed and tell them I have changed its name from Rupert to Jellyrenda and its sex from a boy to a girl...

My mother was unhappy in Carltonville. Afterwards she talked of the ugly bungalow in which we lived, of the constant, threatening presence of the natives, of my father's rough mining friends, who would come to the house late at night, drunk, with my father as coarse as the rest of them. She bore three children, alone, thousands of miles from her own family and distanced from her husband who, although he was asked by the surprisingly enlightened Jewish doctor if he wanted to attend our births, did not, because it was *women's business.*

The isolation frightened her. Next door lived an Afrikaaner woman with an exceptionally beautiful four-year-old daughter. One day, the child had an asthma attack and the woman had to run down the road to ring the hospital. When she got through the matron told her she was being hysterical and refused to send an ambulance. The child died.

My mother armoured herself, turning a serene face towards the world, adapting herself to the role of the loyal wife. She was hurt when others thought her insensible, when her difficulties, because she concealed them, were dealt with brusquely, while other women who were not stoic and who complained were loudly fussed over. When my mother went to South Africa, she was a devout Catholic. By the time she left, she had lost her faith, and I have often wondered how much of the fear which has scarred her life was born then, slouching out of the loneliness and despair which she could not admit because she had to be strong for her little daughters.

She was stern with the black maids, who she said needed to be strictly controlled, and when she found one woman stealing the silver she sacked her immediately. I have never asked her if she saw any parallel between their situation and hers. She bought two Great Danes, for protection, and bred them, so once there were puppies. I also remember a small white terrier called Sally. It concerned the neighbours greatly that I barked before I talked.

Whenever my father was late back from the mine my mother was afraid he was dead. He never rang her to allay her anxiety. Once he was arraigned in a court case on a charge of culpable homicide as a result of a fatal accident, although this is an event of which I know very little. The men lied and he was let off. Maybe that was the sin that closed him off from us, so that he was never there for us in any way we understood as matching our imaginings of him. Our mother filled the gap for us, by telling us he loved us: but later we thought she was a liar, because it seemed to us he didn't.

It isn't true that my father did not love us. But in that love were such failures that he became a lack in our lives, a possibility hovering over a pit of intolerable disappointment, and a lie.

Shortly after the birth of my first son, I was staying at my mother's house in the country. I found a record I remembered from South Africa, songs by a young Miriam Makeba, who was pictured on the front in a long green silk dress. I played it, and as I listened, looking out of the window, I was overcome by an uncontrollable rush of grief. I didn't know why I was weeping, it was old, before I had any words, but it opened within me a vista of pain of which I knew nothing. These stories are what I know of South Africa, but the grief is the truth, and the truth is precisely that which I can't write down, or even think to myself, because I don't know what it is.

Again, when my son was only a few days old, I lay on the bed and watched him sleeping and wondered to myself what it is that babies dream. As I watched him, it was as if a barrier had been removed in my mind and I understood that, if I wanted to, I could remember everything, as if memory was a spool, right back to when I was a baby. So I waited and began to sense a cold wind and darkness rising inside me, inchoate and starless and without hope: and I became frightened and went to the kitchen and made myself some coffee, trying to rid myself of these feelings, already half understanding that they had shaped my present into a hell of emptiness and denial, a hell that my squalling, colicky son, who was driving me past the limits of exhaustion, lay within like a limpid, intolerably fragile flower, my despair and my salvation.

We knew our mother loved us, because she told us so. But the space between her desire to love us and what was given as reality still inhabits us. She loved us, she loved us not. We were aware, in the sadnesses of our flesh, of the secret crevices in her heart, but we had no language to name them. A child without language is a child whose memory is given her, who cannot remember herself. A child without memory is a child without language.

When my mother gave birth to me, she orgasmed.

Those first incandescent flames: a little boy and I squirming on his parents' bed and my thighs and groin and belly luminous with delight. We had no words for what we were doing, it was dark and the dark enfolded us, the bed was like a breast. But my visual memory sees us from the far side of the room, as in a dream when the dreamer looks upon herself from outside, as we were discovered, when I found that what we were doing was shaming, embarrassing, a cause of adult consternation: although I wasn't punished, perhaps I learnt it must be kept secret from everyone, except myself. So, sitting on my potty and feeling my labia, slippery and warm with urine, I took my hand away when I heard my mother's footsteps. That door of pleasure was always open, but only to myself.

I became adept at pleasuring myself. Certain images aroused me: a tiny book, stamped 1812, with worn gilt leather binding, contained a picture of Adam and Eve naked beneath the Tree of Knowledge. I'd lie on my private bed with that picture before my face, bringing myself to the shuddering intensity that already I'd vowed to keep from anyone else, before I had any conscious idea of the mechanics of sex, and none at all of love. By then, perhaps, I had decided that love did not exist.

My childhood was a slaughter of gods.

When my daughter was a very new baby, I had a bath with her. She lay on my breast and I looked at her naked body. I had never seen another cunt before. Sometimes I had examined mine with the aid of a mirror, but what I saw, if it did not disgust me, seemed ugly. When I looked at my daughter, I saw she was a pearl, a flower, a pure syntax of symmetrical beauty. Before then I had never believed my lover's words: they were made in the heat of ardour, pretty compliments to cover an ugliness, politenesses which did not reflect what I knew to be true. Even this word, *cunt*, which I use because there is no other which names, wholly, the complexity of my genitals, is considered an obscene insult. But the meaning of cunt is inflected through usage. Cunt is, must be, innocent and obscene, beautiful and ugly, loving and hostile, a door to life and to death, to consciousness and unconsciousness: it must contain within itself the dark of all authentic pleasure.

I am sometimes afraid, when I lose track of the time, or am unable to account for a missing object, that I am inhabited by another self about whom I know nothing, and who may, if I am not vigilant, overtake my consciousness and commit acts that I consider abhorrent and of which I have no memory. This other sometimes appears in my dreams. It is always a terrifying presence which coldly desires to destroy me. The threat is always physical and always male, but to construe it as an expression of external fears is misleading. I am most afraid of this shadow within myself.

Who is this *I* who writes? I am writing a poem, the poem of myself, and this *I* who writes is and is not the same person who brushes her daughter's hair and sends her to school and does the washing up and sighs heavily before sitting down at her desk. I am the I who obeys the imperatives of the poem, I am a haunting of myself by myself. My meaning will, for the moment, have to inhabit the spaces between these words: you will have to take these sentences and measure them against your own fears, and so gauge my failures.

When we lived in South Africa, when I was a baby, my father was often violent towards my mother. He did not, she said, so much hit her as throw her around when he was drunk. She said she always had bruises down her arms and legs, but she was too ashamed to tell her doctor, who guessed the truth in any case, although he could never get her to admit anything. When they returned to England, the physical violence transmuted into other, more subtle forms of degradation. I did not know this until much later, until I no longer needed that knowledge to release me from my own bruises, my own shame, my own silences, my own fear.

And you, who live in my thoughts, whose presence, lightness and dark, inhabits me, whose tongue loosens the root of my speech: you, whom my blindness illuminates, who take my thread and unwind the labyrinth, who ride me on the waves of my breath, who hand me the six fatal seeds: plough of my heart, my stake of desire, my guide, my murderer: you: whom I know and don't know, inside and utterly separate, speechless and speaking me, traitor and saviour: o absent one, without your faith I am nothing:

Do I kick you under your heart, do I sweat through your skin like a fever, does the air in your mouth smell of my smell, do your hands clench in the shape of me: are you my mask or my shadow or my stripped and shivering flesh, finding its silence at last through the clear note of catastrophe...

VIII Angel

Dawn breaks over the Port of Lisbon, spilling over the harbour's million repeating waves in a welter of azure and gold and eyeblinking silver. The shadow of HMS Fidelis *cuts through this skin of light, revealing the ocean's unsettled depths.*

To the left, we see the sheer ramparts of a fort built flush against the sea, its stone burnished yellow where the new light strikes it, or cool plumpurple where night still lingers. Before and to the right in the distance we see the dim outlines of buildings still veiled in sleep, domes and arches hinting of houses with whitewashed grapeclustered courtyards, and the breeze brings us the faint whiff of horsedung and mansweat and jasmine and attenuated wisp of cockcrow.

On deck, all is motion. The sails strain their rigging in a fresh breeze like councillors readying for oration, chickens poke their squawking flap-combed heads in and out of the coop, seamen with mops and buckets are slopping clean the wooden deck or coiling oiled spirals of rope or crawling with the matchless grace of practice along the yardarms, the Captain paces the bridge up and down with his henchman Mr James, both with their hands folded behind their backs, both talking in undertones, and a crowd of passengers roils like confetti along the rails, facing towards the fort and the shadowed city.

Above the main mast, huge shadowless wings outspread, is an Angel robed in red. Its gold hair and the stuff of its apparel ripple in an air other than that which tosses the hair of the passengers and bellies out the sails. Its slender alabaster hands grip a massive convex mirror.

ANGEL

praise exquisite flesh miraculously smelted from unforgiving elements, hydrogen oxygen nitrogen carbon and intricate mineral mysteries: praise the patience of water linking itself to itself, epthelial, muscular, nervous, connective, contracting, expanding, absorbing, the hundred trillion cells speaking each their chymical sacraments, their opalescent splendour, their divinely asymmetrical equilibrium: praise systemic ritual, bone, muscle, ligament, heart, artery, vein, capillary, lymph, spleen, thymus, lung, diaphragm, stomach, intestine, liver, pancreas, kidney, bladder, ovary, uterus, testicle, urethra, and the lordly endocrine and nerves: praise the particularity of function, the pragmatic morphology of beauty, the sweatbulbs and glandular blossoms breaking open their pheronomic gifts, the flexibility of the hand's twenty seven bones, all skeletal grace levering holding releasing making, the muscular flexion and extension, the proprioceptive explosions, the elasticity of lungs swollen with newly richened blood, the rhythmic contractions of the clitoris, the vagina's violent sheathing, the womb's greedy nose and sperm's urgent fragrance, the epididymal release and the subtle contractions of the glans: praise the transparent skin that grants discreteness and loneliness and death, and love and time and beauty -

Silent and still as an engraving, the Angel holds aloft its mirror, which contains an abstraction of a sky not present in this time and place, an expanse in which all is black save the rose and violet and blind explosive white of elliptical galaxies.

VOICES

I've lost I lost my home my wife I've lost my the secret lost my husband lost I lost my job lost heart lost I've lost my keys lost my children my soul I've lost my way I lost my I lost my mind the secret lost my father fortune lost lover lost sight my brother lost lost I lost I lost my doll I've lost my hope I lost world lost my place lost my life lost

Croneblack shadow with a face like a dish of talcum powder, shockingly rouged on such old skin and pinkrimmed whitelashed boggling blue eyes - poor Mrs Allison poking her index finger through the lattices of the chicken coop, brain like a basket of grasshoppers, hands as fat and smooth as a year-old baby's -

MRS ALLISON

the box is on the ship and the deed is in the box but I've lost the key, what can I do? when I woke up but then it slipped and now what can I do? what was it in the box? looked everywhere up and down and beside and under everywhere and maybe the rooster swallowed it the naughty damned. I'll roast you in hell, a tasty devildinner, it'd be easier than -

Furtively, she sizes up the chances of wringing the rooster's neck unnoticed. The baby hands twitch murderously.

good morning Mrs. Yes, a beautiful - have you seen a key? a box key? around my neck but then maybe the chain slipped or. A beautiful key, a golden shaft and the eye a ruby - thankyou Mrs - thankyou - thankyou -

VOICES

lost - lost -

Blackhaired Michael bound for the Baallarat goldfields presses firm his sensual Celtic mouth and leans his stubborn body against the railings, staring into Lisbon as the hidden dreamer escapes from his shadowed eyes.

MICHAEL

My Jackie my handsome your Michael misses your lips your breath your hair. There's a great bird on the foremast catching the sunrise reminds me of you, how we would laugh! and now all that so long ago like those Roman coins we found in the field. Remember in the church when they read the Song of Songs and I looked over and you was laughing and then you was crying. There's a great yellow castle butting on the sea, we're sailing there and then it's goodbye Europe. My letter goes tonight and my love I see you kissing it and your tears falling. It cost me a shilling for the woman to write it but she wouldn't come down and you'll have to take it to the priest to read my handsome I don't like that his cold white hands and his thin lips saying my love for you and how I can't tell you all the things in my head and my heart like a great furnace blazing with hope for you and me

Out of all the passengers, one only stares directly at the Angel, his mouth exactly the shape of a kiss and two wide blue eyes O O as Agnes shifts him further up her hip, she is tired of grief and tired of poverty and tired of being nothing, she is tired of the sliding and the burden and her face is mottled with his colic and his cough and her fear for him.

AGNES

poor wee cosset what lie will keep thee in this godbrained godbowelled godempty cold the black mouth singing one for one and all alone and two for the coalblack crows on Newgate doorpost and three old ewes knitting at the assizes and four starving dogs trotting down an alley and five dark cottages mum with plague and six the corpses I buried and seven the trumpets to wake them at the end of time

CAPTAIN

One degree port, thankyou, Mr James.

Clouds boil to the surface of the Angel's mirror and dissolve to reveal a great Book closed with a gold clasp. It has no title. An unseen hand opens it and what is written there is perceived as if it is at once seen and heard and inscribed on the heart.

BOOK

Trust my word, seek the grass that is trefoil. Thou knowest the name and art wise and cunning if thou findest it. It is conceived below the earth, born in the earth, quickened in heaven, dies in time, obtains eternal glory

ADELAIDA

It's a mirror but all it shows is blankness.

CAPTAIN

Foresail ho! Three degrees starboard, thankyou, Mr James. Very satisfactory.

ANNA

Dost thou know me, papa?

ADELAIDA

There's a yellow castle, like a dream. Maybe it has gardens full of jasmine and magnolia and little paths that go through and wind back on themselves. The angel will show me and maybe I'll lose myself, maybe I can leave this weight in the gardens, maybe there are monkeys there and they'll take it away to play with and scatter in their houses in the trees

CAPTAIN

Dinah just now reluctantly waking up curling into the warm of the bed with shut eyes and the baby grumbling for the nipple and then into the kitchen where the first light always comes and the children playing on the floor while she cooks them breakfast, her private face, herself as she is, unrelated, unmarried, silent, sufficient, that I will never see, not in all our long years of marriage, except sometimes through a window for a moment, grave and still, writing in her journal, or staring into the moonlight over the sea

ADELAIDA

Then one day maybe something will wake me up, like a prince kissing me in the stories, like a star in a nest of twigs or the light running over a river, and I'll be so hungry and thirsty and empty and it'll be a beast tearing my heart to pieces

ANNA

Nay, I am stranger. I'll know myself no more.

CAPTAIN

On course, Mr James.

The Angel laughs, it is like a cold shower of stars or a fusillade of silver needles.

Briefly Mrs Allison searches through the jugs and drawers and urns of flowers in a villa in Lisbon, turning out the pockets of strangers while they look on in polite and tolerant disbelief...

Mist obscures the mirror and passes and there is Michael, wearing a red neckcloth and filthy white moleskins. His thick black beard

is tangled with clay, and his face is grim with exhaustion. He spills a weight of dark nuggets from a calico bag onto the polished counter of a bank in front of a young man attired in a grey frock coat and spotless white shirt and incongruously frolicsome cravat.

TELLER

Two pounds and three ounces precisely. That works out to - let me see - that works out to one hundred and forty pounds exactly, neither more nor less. You should get into business Mr, er, your day's done, the times are changing. This is going to be a civilised town soon, mark my words. You could buy yourself a suit. Visit a barber. Better yourself. Mark my words, soon the riffraff's going to be cleaned out of here, all the chinks and diggers and the - er, you know, the women of loose - morals - and this will be a place to be proud of, where even a duke could come or the King even, we're not there yet but we don't have to be ashamed of ourselves, there's committees now for the advancement of morals and respectability, you could come now you've got some substance, and help do something about the tone of the place, the tone, Mr er, Mr Thomas, it's the tone that counts -

The teller counts out the last of the money. Michael sweeps it off the counter into his bag and nods pleasantly to the teller.

MICHAEL

Why don't you stick your head up your bum and eat your own shit.

The bank vanishes. In its place is a wooden cottage with a fenced kitchen garden newly planted with herbs and petunias and some straggly saplings, where Agnes bends over a copper of hot water, wringing clothes. At her feet is her baby, now sturdily pulling out tufts of grass from under the copper, bonny and stronglimbed and laughing each time he tumbles over from his tugging.

AGNES

give over now you wee bugger

She hangs the clothes on a line stretched across the garden and the boy totters after her hanging onto her skirt. When she finishes, she snatches him up and blows into the soft skin between his neck and shoulder, before a mist surges over both of them and draws back to reveal Michael again, freshly shaven in a frock coat, cravat, cane, a red carnation in his buttonhole, listening in a room of overdone plushness as a priest reads from a letter. His suit becomes paler and paler as the priest reads until he sits there white from head to foot, with a yellow rose in his buttonhole and lips the colour of a dead man. The room vanishes.

MICHAEL

Forever don't take so long in the end, you think a soul dead as soon as you lose sight of him. Love's a fine idea when it's just a tickle in the ear and some pretty words. But hard to keep true, save for fools like me. I should have died when the roof fell in, like Davey with his hand like a white spider in the clay when we couldn't dig him out in time, or Tom with his lungs full of water and ague and fever screaming for his mam that terrible winter, or maybe I should have just crawled to the bottom of a bottle and drowned there. Bitch.

The surface fills with clouds and against their boiling transformations the Book opens again.

BOOK

they have not hurt me, forasmuch as before him, innocency was found in me

The Book closes and vanishes and again the mirror opens to a black eternal expanse of stars. The Captain looks up from the bridge

and sights the Angel. Suddenly his stern face is illuminated by a smile of rare sweetness.

CAPTAIN

O blessed and devastating presence, Angel of Departure...

IX Accounts

**When I tell my children a story, they always ask me, *Is it true, Mummy?* **And if I say to them, *No, it's only a story*, I feel as if I am lying ...

One weekend we went to the beach. It was a fine day and as we arrived at the foreshore it seemed, although I hadn't visited that beach before, that I had seen it many times: the long yellow sweep of sand stretching to a rocky promontory in the distance, the few people sitting in black pools of shade and the gentle ocean before them pocked with gulls and whitecaps - there are pictures in the National Gallery of exactly this scene, in exactly these colours, painted ninety years ago.

Later in the day we watched the children playing on the rocks. I was tired by then and sat down. There was too much light. The sea was barred with silver and black and the black rocks jutted bluntly out of the water. I could hear the children calling to each other in the distance. I looked down at the rock on which I was sitting and felt suddenly, with an agonising clarity, my exile from my own childhood. While I had been watching the children, I had idly overlaid my perception with my memories of playing among rocks at a beach. But the rock on which I was sitting was alien to my memory. My children were jumping on a tumulus of basalt eroded in curious formations as the sea had worn open the air bubbles in the lava, leaving it rough, and each rock was separated by deep clefts, in which lay sand and tangles of wet seagrass. When I looked up, the memory of the place was of naked black children, shouting and playing as my children were: but I was not there.

The smell was the same: clean volumes of briny wind. We had walked over flat, even turf to reach the rocks, but in my childhood we scrambled down smugglers' paths worn into cliffs, clutching at seapinks and ragged robin, and stood on sand enclosed by high black rocks and watched the waves dash themselves to spray at the point of a small cove. Along the shoreline we found razor shells, the black, spiny egg cases of rays, green seaweed bladdered with tiny air sacs and flat, long lengths of brown kelp. We walked over smooth, brown stones, irregularly scooped to create little pools permanent enough to sustain, as if behind glass, miniature worlds: lacy seaweeds which hid red starfish and crabs and sometimes little fish and the pink spiny sea urchins. Their walls were knobby with limpets and periwinkles and colonies of barnacles and the jellies of sea anemones, which underwater sprouted their bright fleshy tentacles, coral red and shy pink, so I could put my finger in their mouths and feel them close over it, soft and firm and cold.

Often we went to the beach in winter and walked across the deserted sand with the wind cold and tumultuous, dashing the waves against the harsh rocks and sounding over the cliffs towering over us. We'd return home exhilarated and exhausted, and strip off our briny clothes in the porch, which smelt of wet wellington boots and sand, with the dogs jumping up around us; and that night we'd slip effortlessly into sleep and dream of nothing that we remembered.

Or we would visit the wood, its trees cold and bare, its brown earth sprinkled with snow, where we gathered horse chestnuts and painted them gold to hang on the Christmas tree; we walked there in autumn also, for I remember the faint, cold tang of wild strawberries and hazelnuts. A milk-white river, stained with china clay, ran through it, and sometimes there were bluebells and primroses. Its light was quelled like an eye pierced with a knife, when we returned years later and coarse men were axing the trees into the mud and dragging their corpses away.

I remember laneways like green cathedrals with the trees meeting overhead and the black road striped with sunlight and then the open sky of the moors, the yellowing tussocky grass and tumbling stone walls littered with bones of wild goats and ponies, the wind sweeping over with the force of the sea, irresistible and cold, forging out of the blunt granite rocks giant flutes and harps and bowling their voices down to us as we struggled up the hill, our hair flying, and we hid in the crannies and named the rocks - the Chapel, the Whale, the Table - feeling ourselves to be in the throat of something wild and impersonal and raw, indifferent to our presence, splotched and mottled with the lichens of immeasurable age, vast, immoveable, with no purpose except its own blind, inexorable being...

My mother was often happy in England. My father was absent for long periods and she worked alone, bringing up her children and making her home. He would fly to exotic places and return with the little complimentary soaps and bottles of shaving lotion that we loved to play with, and presents: I remember the beautiful turquoise ring, set in a carved gold band, which he gave to my mother. My mother always had lovely rings: black opals and unusual Victorian garnets and a white gold ring set with a light yellow citroen. Later she gave the rings to us, and gradually we lost them. They were stolen or disappeared when we moved house, and now none of those rings which so fascinated us as children remain. All I have is a gold necklace wrought as a cluster of flowers, with a ruby in the centre of each flower, which my father gave to my mother after I was born, and which I will give to my own daughter, when it is time, with the gold ring, also set with a ruby, that was given to me when I had my eldest son. For all their beauty, they are an ambiguous inheritance: for these jewels are gifts of failed love, bequests of sadness and betrayal.

    Now, like my mother, I have three children. Two are sleeping in the next room and the baby is slung on my chest: tonight he is refusing to sleep, he will not release me from the intensity of his presence. He has grown with this writing, beginning with nothing but a seed of desire and gestating in a place inaccessible to light, and now he reveals the tentative shoots of his own, separate mysteries. He was born by candlelight in the bed in which he was conceived. A caul covered his face. His brother and sister came running into the room when he was less than a minute old and even through my pain I registered the awe on their faces.

Eros, the child god, was born of the Earth and the Sky, the third in all creation. What was that mating - hard rock and storm, unforgiving ice over the gentle deltas, boiling air and red lava, the breasts of hills caressed by rain, heat breathing over a naked expanse, the minute kisses of dew? All these, yes, and more, to incarnate the irretrievable risk of love. And what is a child? Its anarchy challenges the world's closed possibilities: are faeces so filthy? is urine so disgusting? is the milk-engorged breast so distasteful? what is a nakedness that is neither shameful nor shameless? and isn't this unorderedness, this unabashed carnality, the unevolved origin of authentic sensation - that is to say, aesthetics?

I still possess editions of *Alice in Wonderland* and *Through the Looking Glass* which I appropriated as mine, although they were expensive books in cases with beautiful reproductions in red ink of the Tenniel illustrations. The dustcovers and cases are long lost, some of the illustrations have extra characters drawn by me and the corner of each page is torn off, as I literally used to eat books when I read them. On the inside page I can trace my reading: there are the wonky capitals I wrote when I first learnt to spell out my name, perhaps before I went to school, with the S backwards; then there is another signing, in smaller, more assured capitals, with my surname, which dates from Carclaze, the first school I attended in St Austell; and lastly a cursive written carefully with fountain pen, from shortly after we arrived in Australia.

I loved Carclaze. Every morning I would cross a little sharply angled street where a lollipop man would halt the traffic and walk up the road to the red brick building. I had a leather satchel and a special green drawstring bag with "A" sewn on it for my elevenses. The school entrance had wide stone steps with low walls either side and church-shaped doors which embraced me as I entered. Learning was easy for me. My teacher was a lanky, tall woman with glasses and iron-grey hair caught in a bun. I can remember the pleasure I felt in attaining mastery over the simple books we were given to read, a pleasure that later extended to a fascination with codes and inventing fantastic scripts and languages. It was a simple pleasure, simply felt, one a sportsman might feel who has a ball obeying without conscious thought the direction of his mind and body, an effortless sense of rightness and confidence.

In rare moments I can still feel this pleasure in its naive first sense, the conviction of a leverage which could topple anything. Writing is possible only because this remnant of childish omnipotence persists through all the dulling failures of adulthood. Yet if it were not for these shaping and devastating failures, if that omnipotence still lay within the width of my hand, the desire to write may not exist.

When as a child you first read a book, there are mountains and forests and lakes, and they are all real, as real as your hand turning the pages, more real than the narrowing world which bars your perceptions with its prohibitions of time and space and convention: and in the fabulous stories which unfold before you their mysteries, the legible mysteries which reveal the colour of a single leaf and the precise sound of a pebble rolling in the stream of a mountain you have never seen, the hiddenness and incomprehensibility of your life is translated into a seed which lies beneath the surface of the warm, imagined earth, which remains hidden and enclosed, which itself will never flower into comprehensibility but conceals in its nascence all that is unrevealed in the explicit fantasy of the story: the truth which is planted there, inexpressible in any other way.

I cannot understand myself except through language. This is a misfortune: there are better, simpler and more direct ways of understanding. They are the spaces of silence which we inhabit fully, the epiphanies which are always Edenic, which language struggles so hard to enter and, in doing so, exiles us from the garden. And yet, in its trespass, a poetic language retrieves the unanaesthetised reality we inhabit at our births, and reminds us that, in its perpetual destruction and restoration of language, in its serious play and playful seriousness, in its derangement of dualities and smashing of unities, in its acceptance and rejection of mortality and finitude, poetry is nothing if it is not a making of love.

...*beauty is nothing,* sang Rilke, *but this terrifying beginning...* The terror of beauty is that *everything* is beautiful. It is the chaotic self, the chaotic body, the chaotic world, fragmentary, diffuse, unassigned to meaning, against which form, an aesthetic armour, a self by which we understand our given selves, defends itself from the chaos within and without it. And art contains the terror of obliteration, which inhabits the centre of beauty. It admits the reality of death, of human finitude and failure, it admits that the world is not us and that we do not control it. This admission is love: the voluntary renunciation of self-tyranny, the ascension to the place of ordinary beauty, which redeems nothing.

In the gardens of childhood, there is no time.

Time begins suddenly.

I am looking at a picture in a magazine. It is a black and white photograph of earth which is crazed by drought. The cracks are so black they seem bottomless, as if they might open to the heart of the world, and the earth is completely naked and stretches to a far horizon. Otherwise there is only sky. The picture fills me with inchoate terror: it has no scale and I imagine falling through the gaps. The cracks open in my dreams, the earth rings like a great hollow bell, tolling a mysterious horror.

This is the place we are going to. Suddenly the fact is firmly fixed in our lives. We will be away for three years in Australia, where the days and nights are upsidedown and the seasons are backwards. My mother is desperately unhappy. We will travel without my father on the ship, because he is flying over there in an aeroplane, and she will leave behind her, with a month's notice, the home she has so lovingly created. Three years is unimaginable: it is half of my life. Perhaps we sense that we will never come back, that the house is already becoming as insubstantial as memory, perhaps we know that we will walk the woods only in our dreams, that the taste of wild hazelnuts and strawberries will haunt our palates like a forgotten language, that, after this, we will belong nowhere.

God is loosening, like a dying tooth.

We are packing shadows into boxes. They live in the bow-fronted chest of drawers and the mahogany sideboard, nestling between the shelves; they hide beneath the beds and in the wardrobes and behind the cushions on the sofa; they huddle with the spiders in the curtains and corners of the cupboards; they are bedded down in velvet with the silver; they slide at night behind our dressing gowns hanging from the bedroom door; they snuffle in the spaces behind the oven and the fridge; they warm themselves inside our empty clothes and curl up in our shoes to sleep; they are folded inside the sheets and towels and blankets; they are stowed inside wooden boxes and our name is stamped on them and they are taken away.

We are on a train: we are in a hotel room. There is a narrow bathroom at the end of a gloomy passage. We go to the zoo and see the white entrance gates: we stand outside a palace and watch the guards on their horses: we walk down a flight of steps into the waxworks and see the red light flickering over Nelson's death at Trafalgar.

We are at the docks. There are multitudes of people and a huge white ship called the *Orcades*. There is a gangplank shifting slightly on the dock. Our father comes with us to the ship and puts our luggage in the cabin. Everything is very small: the beds are narrow bunks and there is scarcely any floor. A tiny bathroom leads off the cabin. Our porthole is level with the sea and the waves splash over it. There is a smell of brine and fresh paint.

We are standing on the deck, leaning over the painted rails. We are waving. On either side of us, everyone is waving. On the dock, my father is waving, my grandparents, my uncles and aunts and cousins. The gangplank is carried up on deck, the rope is cast off, the tugboats are pulling us out into the harbour. The green choppy water opens between us and the dock: suddenly it is much, much wider, suddenly we are loosed from the shore. We are still waving at the people on the dock, but we can no longer distinguish their faces: we can no longer separate their bodies from the knots of colour on the quay: they are smaller and smaller: and then they are gone.

X Apeiron

From the private journal of Captain Adam Asterion, discovered in a box of great antiquity sold recently at auction in Melbourne, Australia. The box, carved of ebony and inlaid with gold and ivory, bears the motifs of a snake and a bull emblazoned on a depiction of the sun, with the moon in its four phases in each corner. The key, worked in gold, is charmingly shaped as a snake with ruby eyes. Although the materials are exotic, the method of abstraction is characteristically Bronze Age Celtic. The voyage of the HMS Fidelis *in 1869 is noted in official records as uneventful, apart from the death of one passenger from natural causes; the ship docked at Melbourne on September 18th, 1869, with a complement of 133 passengers and crew, and six convicts bound for Van Diemans Land.*

June 16th 1869 Lat: 39°N Long: 10°E Conditions: Exceptionally Fine. Wind NNW, 5 knots. Successful negotiation past the Cabo de Roca into the Bay of Lisbon at Dawn. As we were gathering in the topsail all looked upwards and were much struck by the sight of an Angel illuminated by the first rays of light. It was balancing on the main mast, above the Crow's-Nest, lifting its voice in a song of indescribable melody. Several conversions were reported immediately among the passengers and crew to a variety of religions, most commonly Sufism and Bhuddism, but also to branches of Christianity, in particular Greek Orthodoxy, the Pentecostal Church and Roman Catholicism. I am at a loss to explain the idiosyncratic nature of this phenomenon, since it appears completely unrelated to Nationality, but I fear lest sectarian wars break out among the populace of the Ship. Others among the passengers and crew reported they saw only a great Bird, perhaps an Albatross, although such birds are seldom seen so far South, which has caused the major Dissension so far. For my part, I find such Visitations have an unsettling ambiguity, since such Beings do not understand a Human measure, but weigh an ant and a mountain the same on the scales of their Cosmologie. Yet the Beauty of its Face and Apparel was such that I should not have cared to miss the Phenomenon, whatever the Consequences of its appearance. *Fidelis* will dock in Lisbon for three days, conditions permitting, taking on water and supplies, disbursing some five Passengers and taking on three. After that, we will be stepping from known Civilisation into the Unknown. It is always a time of trepidation as much as excitement, no matter how often one repeats the experience.

(. . .)

June 30th 1869 Lat 35°N Long 18°W. Conditions continuing exceptionally fine, SW 15 knots. Standing off the Canary Islands. The crew is in excellent Morale and Health, despite the bizarre flowering of Devotions amidst the Ship; for the moment I have chosen to ignore the behaviour, except when it intrudes on Discipline. Most adhere to their normal routines, apart from the seaman who demanded to be watch on the first Bell so he could make the morning Prayer call from the Crow's-Nest; however, since another of the seamen rolled out his prayer mat in a fit of ecstatic Devotion from one of the yard arms, thus falling twenty feet and breaking his arm and causing much disorder among the foresails, he has desisted. I must confess I am much bored with talk of God. I would take up Atheism out of sheer Perverseness if it were not as pernicious as any other Dogma. Perhaps one minor matter has augmented my Jaundice: the new cook from Lisbon is devoting his culinary Imaginings to allegories of the Scriptures. Unfortunately he confines his most ambitious Endeavours to the Officers. Last night we had whale meat in which he had stuffed olives (signifying the Holy Land) and three grains of rice (signifying the days and nights in which Jonah lay in the whale's belly). The whole was covered with pastry, to symbolise the sackcloth in which the citizens of Nineveh demonstrated their piety to the Lord. This was followed by a Pumpkin Syllabub, recalling the gourd with which the Lord admonished Jonah for his anger. I can only say that I wish it had fallen to me, that I might have vomited on dry land: for seasickness has long been a stranger to me and I am the better for the estrangement. Religions serve often as troublesome dividers of Humanity, but to attack a man with his Vittles is a gruesome Evolution. I am hoping a stern dressing down will inhibit his Piety and allow him to contemplate a plain Roast without spiritual Misgivings.

Our complement of Convicts is causing little trouble, apart from a certain Anna Keyes, whom the Ship's Physician contemplates in despair and fascination. I have done all I can to ensure their condition is as Humane as possible, given the limitations of their transportation in one of the meanest spaces on this Vessel, which is necessitated for reasons of Security and to fulfil the obligations due to His Majesty's Government. Miss Keyes behaves as if she were chained hand and foot, as if it were a Hundred years before. She refuses to wash or to eat except for the bare minimum required to sustain life and when questioned will only speak of the murder of her father, for which she believes she has suffered the fate of Transportation. This is not borne out by her Records, which state she is convicted for repeated transgressions such as petty theft and prostitution. Yet Dr Toogood tells me she is a woman of Education and has established that her life of Crime began with the death of a child born out of Wedlock and her subsequent Banishment from her family. He is convinced she is salvageable, but fears her future as a Convict will fail to ensure this, since Compassion is not a marked feature of much of the penal system.

We are in the phase of the Full Moon and I must confess, no matter how many times I have witnessed it, I never tire of the sight of the Moon rising over a calm sea. She appears in State, robed in gold and with a long train of silver which runs from the horizon to the Ship; and such is the solemnity and grace of her aspect, in the immense silence and solitude of the Ocean, that her rising creates a stillness within my Soul, which basks in her yet more still Beauty, untroubled, if even for this short eternity, by the pangs of mortal Desire.

(. . .)

August 8th (?) Lat: Equatorial. Long: Uncertain. Conditions: Becalmed.
It is some days since I have been able to keep any kind of Record, because we have been afflicted by a severe Storm. The last date I can ascertain is the thirty first of July, when at about sunset a black cloud was noted on the East horizon, coming with an irresitibible rapidity towards the Ship. It looked like a great black Tiger as it approached us, its paw lashing the Ocean into a tumult visible even from a great Distance. I ordered all sails lashed and everything battened down; we had scarce finished when the storm was upon us, surpassing in its Extremity everything I have heretofore experienced. Its initial strike was a wave which appeared as a Mountain, towering at least two hundred feet above the mast; by some Miracle the ship was not knocked over. In the first wash of water over the deck we lost one passenger, a Mr Adams, who had disobeyed orders and had inexpertly lashed himself to the mast, unnoticed until it was too late in the rush to prepare the Ship. We also lost many supplies and provision, including the chicken coop. It is hard to tell how long we were born on the wings of this storm: there was no way of telling day from night, the Darkness was all encompassing, but I should estimate about seven days. I have no way of describing how the ship weathered it; each moment was of constant vigilance in the midst of a chaos of Hell, and fear lest the vigilance should fail and our fates be overwhelmed in the Deep. I did not sleep the entire time, and indeed Sleep, in the intolerable howling of the wind, the fearsome cracking and groaning of the Ship's timbers, the unendurable cold, and the unceasing anxiety, would have been nigh impossible, had I had any choice. For all that time my entire faculties were concentrated on the necessity of Survival, for the merest flicker of inattention would have meant the loss, not only

of my life, but of each one of the one hundred and thirty nine Souls aboard this Vessel. In a sense, it was as if all our Souls were one Soul. I did not have time to feel Terror, as no doubt was suffered by those pent in the cabins, in total Darkness because it was possible to light no fires. The storm departed as quickly as it arrived, having carried us off-course to an extent I cannot Determine, for reasons I will explain at another time. We are now becalmed in waters as still as were previously Violent. I set a watch and retired to my cabin, where I slept for approximately twenty hours without once stirring; I woke up with my limbs in the same position as I when I flung them on my bunk. I am still empty with exhaustion and feel almost too tired to eat and at this moment cannot bear the thought of the monstrous Effort it will take to restore order on the ship. By some Miracle none of the masts have snapped, although there are some hurts to the yard arms and sails. Considering the severity of the Forces to which we have been subjected, the damage is surprisingly minimal. There is much that is broken and much that is lost, but the vessel is still intact. *Fidelis* is taking on water from a so far untraced leak, which requires four men constantly at the pumps to mitigate, but that is the only structural damage.

August 9th, position as before, conditions as before. We cannot determine our position because the Ship's Compass was struck by lightning during the Storm and no longer functions, continuously twirling as if the Ship itself were spinning like a Top. Moreover, the stars are unrecognisable. No chart I possess contains such Constellations, which burn unnaturally huge and still. Whereas two days ago we feared we'd freeze to death, now we are in danger of boiling alive: it is as if the Sea were a giant frying pan and we some unwary Insects marooned on a leaf in its oil. There is no escape from the Heat; on deck the brightness is unbearable, beneath is all foetid and airless. I guess we are near the Equator because of the Sun, but this seems, really, a futile guess: we have been blown off the Map. I have no way of estimating even what Ocean we are in. I have instigated rationing of Water and Food, and have placed a guard over the water to deter thieves, since the Temperature is such that one is continuously thirsty. Only Night brings relief from the heat, and generates some curious Phenonoma: strange lights, like silks of scarlet, azure, emerald and purple, hang in Folds over the horizon. The water itself glints with a Phosphorescence, which glitters on the sluggish edges of the waves or in brief trails beneath them, marking perhaps the passage of some creature of the ocean, or breaks in a brief wave of sparks when the Flying Fish, common in this region, skim across the glassy surface of the sea.

August 10th, position as before, conditions as before. There is beginning to be Unrest on the Ship, due to the unrelenting Monotony and Heat and its associated Privations. It was distracted momentarily by the apparition of a Albatross, which lighted on the main mast. Its appearance was greeted with both cheers and curses, depending on the kind of Luck with which each Soul credited it. I am encouraged because it must mean we are not so far from some kind of Land. The only apparent occurence in this cursed Zone is the Rising and the Setting of the Sun.

August 11th, position as before, conditions as before. A sighting of what looked to be a school of Porpoises at a distance of perhaps two or three miles off our starboard side. When I focused the Eyeglass, it looked to me as if there were young Maidens playing in the Ocean, each with a silver tail. I said nothing of this to Mr James, to whom I passed the eyeglass, and he said nothing of it to me.

August 12th, position as before, conditions as before.

August 13th, as above.

August 14th, as above. The relentless Heat continues Exhausting.

August 15th, as above. Some of our Complement are exhibiting signs of Melancholia and Derangement. I feel helpless to mitigate their ill Humours, being little better Myself. I am Instigating greater

Discipline upon the Ship in an effort to combat these possibly dangerous Developments. This is generating some Hostility amidst the Passengers, which is Unfortunate. In the Immense silence of the Ocean, it is possible to hear the Convicts screaming at night, which is Conducive to Irrational thoughts; I have ordered their Release from their Prison, there being little chance of their Escape here.

August 16th, position as before, conditions as before.

August 17th, position as before, conditions as before.

August 18th, position as before, conditions as before. If this Situation continues, the populace of the Ship will be in the Grip of Insanity. Such motionlessness is Intolerable; each night the sun sinks Bloodily into the Sea and each night every Eye is fixed on the Horizon, fermenting with Envy: for He alone is able to Move. I am in constant Anxiety each hour, that something will explode: minor disagreements and bickerings are here Magnified, so as to make the smallest Slight as incendiary as Gunpowder. I am only able to Contain the threat by Discipline: but before long I fear that Mutinous Thoughts will overtake my Will and leave us to the mercy of Anarchy.

August 19th, position as before, conditions as before. A disturbance today: one of the Passengers, a certain Michael Thomas, shot the Albatross for a Bet with one of the other Passengers. To shoot such a Bird is folly in the best of circumstances; in a position such as ours, where all is Dolorous Uncertainty and our fate lies at the whim of some Unknown Force, such an act is one of Criminal Stupidity. The corpse still lies on the Deck, its wings stretched out the length of a Man, with the wound in its Head like an ugly Accusation. I was forced to prevent a Brawl between a group of Passengers and the Crew, who were likely to murder Mr Thomas in their fear and incredulity and anger. For myself, tonight I am sick at heart and beset by Despairs. I do not know how long I will be able to maintain discipline on the Ship, although Discipline is the only means by which we will avoid the derangement which attends us being so Lost. I have half the crew holystoning the deck half the day already and once all the sails are mended, the barrels caulked, all objects stowed and order completely restored, I shall face the problem of Boredom among the crew, which already is Demoralised by the Heat and our Unnatural stillness. The passengers are another Problem altogether; there are some, women and men, of dubious morals amongst them and enforced Idleness may cause who knows what kind of explosions. Moreover, I am personally afflicted by intolerable Longing for Dinah and the children; the thought plagues me that I shall never see them again, shall never again be restored to the Haven of my family. Each Departure carries with it this risk, but I have never felt the grief of this Possibility so keenly. Today I saw little Bessie in front of me on the deck, reaching up her arms towards me: I bent to pick her up, as naturally as if she were there, and were not some phantom of my Imagination, but she vanished. Dinah is speaking to me at night before I sleep; I could swear to her presence. Such Visions are briefly comforting but turn soon into Torments; they remind me piercingly of my Love for them and simultaneously of our Distance, which now, in this place of unmapped Stars and unpredictable Phenomena, seems beyond the possibility of return.

August 20th, as before. In an attempt to propitiate the sin of Murdering the Albatross, today we had a formal Funeral. It was a peculiar business altogether, since there were so many Religions to take into Account; and once again I had to Mediate hostilities to prevent the possibility of another Funeral. Also, many aboard grumbled it was a Nonsense or even a Blasphemy to attend a mere Bird this way; but since there is nothing to do, the activity attracted the attention of most on the Ship. In a strange way, it was a moving ceremony; the corpse was lashed in canvas and weighted with lead and sank with a surprising swiftness to the unseen depths of the Ocean as the most Ecumenical Hymn we could think of, Blake's *The Fly*, was sung by a motley of inharmonious voices.

August 21st, position unknown. A strange Occurence today, although strange Occurences now might be said to be Commonplace. Although there is still no breath of air to fill the Sails, the Ship started to move. After our initial surprise we ascertained this was due to some Current beneath the Ship, carrying us forward at about 10 knots in what we presume to be a SE direction (although it may be NW, since we have no Way of establishing our Bearings). Since almost anything is better than the awful Inanition of the last few days, the morale of the Ship has lightened, but I am weighted down by Dread of the possibilities which await us. Perhaps our absurd Ceremony yesterday instigated this change in our Fortunes, but it seems to me that to assume our Salvation is a vain Presumption. Nothing is known of this Sea; it is utterly strange to me and obeys Laws which might be said to be Supernatural, or at least outside the ordinary ken of Mariners. We tried rowing out of the current, but it has the Vessel fast in its motion, as if we were in the grip of a giant Fist; and since we have no choice of our direction, there is nothing to do but follow it and do our best to manage with Honour intact whatever we find to be our Fate.

August 27th, position unknown. For days now we have been borne on this strange current. It is now cooler and we have moved out of the region of Phosphorescence, but the Sun is not behaving in any way I recognise: or at least, it is still in a Position to suggest we are in Equatorial regions. We have observed no Land, although I keep a constant Lookout. Supplies are beginning to look very grim; we are all existing on quarter rations, with a month's supply in hand at this rate, and I have doubled the guard over the food and water. Midshipman Ranter was caught redhanded stealing some meat; the punishment devised for him by Mr James was unique. He had him tied to the foremast all day, with the offending meat tied around his neck, while the rest of the Crew periodically rubbed his face with it. It was, I think, rather more cruel than a knock with the belaying pin; but I hope it deters further Thieving. This relentless Motion is in many ways as Disturbing as continuous Calm; the speed is without any Variation. And the Uncertainty of our Destination preys on my mind like a Voracious Beast.

August 28th. Now it has become clear where the current was leading us. At 8.15 hours the current began to hasten, as if it was reaching its Destination. Within a matter of minutes we were running at 15 knots, then 20 knots, then 25; the Ship began to shudder beneath the Strain of its speed and I feared for its Soundness. At the same time, a noise of Thunder and an unidentifiable Whistling or Howling became audible, increasing with our speed. I sent all beneath Deck apart from Myself and Mr James, since despite the Danger of the situation it seemed wiser to take precautions. We lashed ourselves to the Mast, preparing for the Unknown, and commended our souls and the souls of those Within to God. Within a short space of time the Source of the Noise and the mysterious Current became evident. I have heard of such things. A giant Whirlpool, or Maelstrom, the size of a large lake, was open in the Ocean, drawing our fragile Craft irresistibly into its Mouth. Despite my terror I was unable to overcome a feeling of astonishment and Awe that such things should be: I have never before beheld the Majesty and Power of the Elements in such naked Force and Beauty. Above the Maelstrom the spray of the water drawn and smashed therein made a Rainbow of exceptional Brightness and Clarity, which hung in the sky as if it were a banner of Welcome. The Ship was now proceeding at a rate which I estimate to be more than 70 knots and was still accelerating. We came to the Lip of the Maelstrom and Mr James and I looked for the first time down into an Abyss of a Depth our eyes could not trace. It looks to pierce the very Heart of the World. The whole Ship leaned over at an angle of 180° but, because of the centrifugal force, nothing on deck shifted. Then, with a Great Shudder, we were over the Lip and in the current of the whirlpool itself. Immediately it was as if Night descended upon Us; if we look upwards, we can see the stars in an unnaturally azure Sky, framed by a great Wall of Turbulent Waters. But on the Ship itself, it is as if we are in the midst of a Great Stillness. There is nothing for us to do now; no seamanship within my knowledge can draw us out of this Phenomenon. I gave the order for all to come on Deck and never have I seen a crowd of People at once so frightened and awestruck; their Silence was complete. All differences between us are Dissolved; our fate is Common and Absolute. All at once, with no Promptings, each of us started singing the 23rd Psalm. By its end, I confess without Shame that I was weeping. Once again, I saw before me, as if they were Present, my Family; if I could have embraced them at that Moment, I am sure my Heart should have shattered its Bonds and broken Intirely. I am now beyond all rational Hope of ever holding them in my Arms again. Yet, despite my Despair and Grief, I am possessed by strange Exhilaration, which I am at a loss to explain, as if everything I desire and is Mine is before me, as behind a door which is merely closed and presently will Open: and I am overwhelmed with Gratitude for the beauty and terror of the World...

At this point, the Journal ends.